Which One Was The Real Nick Clayton?

The man her sister had described, or the one Lexi herself had observed?

There was no way you could call Nick irresponsible or callous. She could not imagine him knowingly abandoning his son or telling the boy's mother to get out of his life.

And most devastating of all was Lexi's sense of guilt for her personal involvement with the very man she had come to confront. What was she to believe? Her sister's accusations, or her own observations of a man who made her tingle with excitement and caused her heart to sing?

Dear Reader,

Hey, look us over—our brand-new cover makes Silhouette Desire look more desirable than ever! And between the covers we're continuing to offer those powerful, passionate and provocative love stories featuring rugged heroes and spirited heroines.

Mary Lynn Baxter returns to Desire and locates our November MAN OF THE MONTH in the *Heart of Texas,* where a virgin heroine is wary of involvement with a younger man.

More heart-pounding excitement can be found in the next installment of the Desire miniseries TEXAS CATTLEMAN'S CLUB with *Secret Agent Dad* by Metsy Hingle. Undercover agent Blake Hunt loses his memory but gains adorable twin babies—and the heart of lovely widow Josie Walters!

Ever-popular Dixie Browning presents a romance in which opposites attract in *The Bride-in-Law.* Elizabeth Bevarly offers you *A Doctor in Her Stocking,* another entertaining story in her miniseries FROM HERE TO MATERNITY. *The Daddy Search* is Shawna Delacorte's story of a woman's search for the man she believes fathered her late sister's child. And a hero and heroine are in jeopardy on an island paradise in Kathleen Korbel's *Sail Away.*

Each and every month, Silhouette Desire offers you six exhilarating journeys into the seductive world of romance. So make a commitment to sensual love and treat yourself to all six!

Enjoy!

Joan Marlow Golan
Senior Editor, Silhouette Desire

Please address questions and book requests to:
Silhouette Reader Service
U.S.: 3010 Walden Ave., P.O. Box 1325, Buffalo, NY 14269
Canadian: P.O. Box 609, Fort Erie, Ont. L2A 5X3

The Daddy Search
SHAWNA DELACORTE

Silhouette® Desire®

Published by Silhouette Books

America's Publisher of Contemporary Romance

SILHOUETTE BOOKS

ISBN 0-373-76253-4

THE DADDY SEARCH

Copyright © 1999 by SKDennison, Inc.

Visit us at www.romance.net

Printed in U.S.A.

Books by Shawna Delacorte

Silhouette Desire

Yours Truly

SHAWNA DELACORTE

has delayed her move to Washington State, staying in the Midwest in order to spend some additional time with family. She still travels as often as time permits, and is looking forward to visiting several new places during the upcoming year while continuing to devote herself to writing full-time.

Prologue

"There's nothing more to say, Mother. Nick Clayton is Jimmy's father and he has to pay for deserting Marnie when he found out she was pregnant. You're not going to talk me out of it. I'll be leaving for Jackson Hole, Wyoming, first thing in the morning."

Lexi quickly concluded her phone conversation, then went into the living room where her five-year-old nephew had plopped down in the middle of the floor to watch television. She studied him a moment as she pulled her long blond hair into a ponytail and fastened it with a rubber band. He had his mother's looks—Marnie's light brown hair and blue-gray eyes. Friends and family had always said if it hadn't been for Marnie being six years older than Lexi, the two girls would have looked enough alike to have been mistaken for twins. Both girls were tall and slender, and they wore the same size clothes.

Marnie had been a good mother. What she and her son

lacked in material possessions Marnie had made up for in love and attention. It was almost as if she had searched all her life for someone who needed her, someone to whom she could give her love, and she had found what she'd been seeking when her son was born. Marnie's death had created a tragic upheaval in Jimmy's life and left a void that Lexi tried hard to fill. A touch of sadness washed over her, but it boosted her resolve to see things through to the conclusion.

"Jimmy?" The little boy looked up at the sound of her voice. "I have some business that I need to take care of...out of town. You'll be staying with Grandma for a little while. And while you're there, she's going to take you to the zoo." Lexi forced an encouraging smile and tried to make her voice sound upbeat and casual, as if nothing were wrong. "Won't that be fun?"

Lexi set about packing a suitcase for Jimmy and then packed for her own trip. She was determined and her mother was opposed and that's the way it had been from the moment Lexi first mentioned the idea four months ago, immediately following her sister's death. Neither of them had budged from their positions and Lexi had decided to proceed with her plan. She needed to secure Jimmy's future while trying to make sense of what had happened.

Even though Marnie's death was technically an accident, Lexi still held Nick Clayton responsible. Marnie had been forced to take on a second job to provide for her son. It was on her way to that second job, driving through a deluge when everyone had been warned to stay off the roads, that she had been caught in a flash flood and drowned. Now Lexi had to raise her sister's five-year-old son. Lexi loved Jimmy as much as if he had been her own child, and she was prepared to confront the man Marnie said had gotten her pregnant, then refused to accept any responsibility. She was going to demand that this unprincipled man contribute to Jimmy's upbringing and see to it that the little boy received a good education. Yes, indeed—Lexi fully intended to confront Nick Clayton.

Then the nagging little thought surfaced again—the one that questioned if it was possible for this to be yet another of Marnie's exaggerations. Lexi shoved the disturbing notion aside. Surely Marnie wouldn't have lied about something this important…surely not.

One

Lexi stared blankly out the window at the passing scenery as the shuttle van made its way along the road. The other passengers were laughing and happy, obviously looking forward to a fun-filled holiday. But not Lexi. Fun was the very last thing on her mind. She leaned back in her seat and closed her eyes in an attempt to ease the tension headache that throbbed at her temples.

She went over the facts for what seemed like the hundredth time in the past four months. She recited them in her mind almost like a litany. Marnie had met Nick Clayton while vacationing at the Clayton's Via Verde Dude Ranch. They had an affair that included a trip to Hawaii where she became pregnant. When Marnie told Nick, he refused to accept any responsibility. Not knowing what else to do, Marnie had confided to Lexi and finally told their mother, Colleen, that she was pregnant and the father had deserted her.

Colleen had blamed her daughter, saying it was just one more example of Marnie's wild and irresponsible behavior to add to an already long list. Marnie and Lexi's father had died ten years ago. Being widowed at such a young age left their mother an embittered woman. Since then, their relationship with their mother could best be described as adversarial, which only made the strained situation worse. Lexi had tried her best to be supportive, but Colleen had informed Marnie that she could not look to her for any help with this latest mess of hers. An angry Lexi wanted to confront Nick Clayton and threaten him with legal action, but Marnie had begged her not to, so Lexi reluctantly agreed to defer to her sister's wishes.

Marnie wanted to have the baby. When Jimmy was born, Marnie had signed a document stating if anything happened to her, she wanted her sister to be her son's legal guardian rather than their mother. Marnie had eventually reconciled with her mother but had never gotten around to changing the document. So, with Marnie's unexpected death, Lexi had become Jimmy's guardian with her mother there to help care for the boy.

And now, four months later and against her mother's strong objections, Lexi had taken all her savings and spent it on a three week stay at an expensive Wyoming dude ranch—certainly not the type of place she normally would have associated with her sister's interests. She intended to confront the man she held responsible, even though indirectly, for her sister's death. But first she needed to check things out in person, determine for herself exactly who this Nick Clayton was. Lexi had never felt so emotionally exhausted, or as old beyond her twenty-six years, as she did at this moment.

The van turned into a long, tree-lined driveway, then came to a halt in front of a large building. "Welcome to

Via Verde Dude Ranch, folks, here in the heart of beautiful Jackson Hole, Wyoming. I'll have your luggage unloaded in just a minute.'' The driver busied himself with suitcases as the passengers climbed out of the van.

Lexi took in her surroundings. The grounds were attractively landscaped and the buildings all had an appropriately rustic look, contributing to the overall atmosphere of the dude ranch. She also noted two tennis courts, several tree-shaded terraces and a large swimming pool with a children's wading pool and a Jacuzzi.

Then her gaze landed on the corral, her attention drawn by a highly spirited horse being led into a chute. She wandered over to the fence so she could get a better look at what was happening. Leaning against the railing, she watched as a cowboy climbed into the chute, then eased himself onto the back of the agitated horse. His hat blocked her view of his face, but his broad shoulders, long legs and the snug fit of his jeans told her the rest of him certainly warranted closer scrutiny. The chute gate sprang open and the snorting bronco shot out into the corral. It appeared that she had arrived just in time to get a glimpse of a mini rodeo.

The cowboy's hat flew off, revealing a man of about thirty with dark hair and handsome features...*very* handsome features. Her thoughts drifted for a brief moment. There was certainly a lot to be said about the appeal of the rugged Wild West and the equally rugged men who lived there. She returned her attention to the action in the corral. The rider appeared to have the upper hand, but not for long. The unruly horse leaped into the air, twisted half around, then threw the rider off its back.

Lexi flinched. The cowboy hit the ground with a thud that nearly jarred her bones in sympathy with his plight. She watched him brush the dirt from his jeans, then rub his well-formed backside where he had landed. She toyed with the notion that kissing whatever he had bruised and making it well just might be a delightful way to pass the time—certainly a tantalizing idea that fitted perfectly with this drop-dead gorgeous cowboy. Her breathing quickened. She had no idea the Wild West could be so...so *entertaining*.

Then this prime physical specimen grabbed his hat from the ground and walked straight toward her. He exuded an undeniable sexuality wrapped in a layer of rugged masculinity—a very potent combination for sure. A little twinge of embarrassment poked at her. It was almost as if he had read her thoughts and come over to grant her the errant wish—a tempting possibility that produced a heated surge of desire where this virile man was concerned.

She noted the way he moved—a walk that was not a swagger and showed no arrogance, yet clearly defined the essence of a man full of confidence about who he was, where he was going and what he wanted out of life. All in all, a very attractive and appealing package that could easily set any woman's heart aflutter, and she was no exception. Then a dash of cold water dampened her thoughts as she recalled exactly why she was at the ranch. Fantasizing about a sexy cowboy should have been the last thing on her mind.

As he drew closer, he appeared even more good-looking than he had from a distance. And then he smiled—a cross between a sexy come-hither look and one of open warmth—showing perfect white teeth made all the more noticeable by his golden tan. She wasn't sure, but she thought he might be the most devastatingly handsome man she had ever seen...just the type to cause a woman to have delicious fantasies of a truly erotic nature.

She took a deep breath as the warmth swept through her body. She could almost feel his bare skin against hers, hear the ragged breathing of someone enveloped in the throes of passion.

A touch of surprise tempered her wandering thoughts. This certainly was not like her, conjuring up such heated fantasies about a stranger regardless of how attractive she found him. She was much more pragmatic than that. She suddenly felt like a teenager with raging hormones. True, she hadn't been on a date since taking responsibility for Jimmy, but that didn't excuse such totally off-the-wall and inappropriate musings where this stranger was concerned. She again reminded herself of the very serious purpose that had brought her to the ranch and the task she had set for herself. Meeting an exciting man was not part of that agenda, regardless of the sensual magnetism drawing her into his realm.

He came to a halt not more than five feet from her, removed his leather work gloves and tucked them into his belt. His brilliant blue eyes seemed to penetrate right into her existence and hold her soul captive. She had no idea who he was, but she was certainly anxious to find out. If she had known dude ranches offered up such delectable talent, she would have visited one a long time ago.

Then he spoke, the sound of his voice sending a tremor of excitement through her body while drawing her even farther into his magnetic aura.

"Hi. I don't believe I've seen you around here before." He reached out and tugged at her sunglasses until he had removed them to reveal her entire face. "That's much better. Now I'm sure I haven't seen you around here." He handed the sunglasses back to her. "You really shouldn't hide those beautiful eyes behind these dark glasses."

"Oh?" She tried to fall in line with his open, easy manner. "You mean you don't think they lend an air of mystery?"

He ignored her question. "I hope you realize you're responsible for that horse tossing me to the ground."

She felt her eyes widen in shock at his accusatory words. "Me? What did I do?"

"You appeared from out of nowhere and stood there looking like the most intriguing woman I'd ever seen— hair of spun gold and half your face covered by these large dark glasses. By the time I got my mind back on the fact that the horse and I had different goals, it was too late. I was on my backside in the dirt wondering what happened." He flashed a sexy yet nonthreatening smile. "So you now owe me something to make up for this terrible inconvenience."

"Oh?" She couldn't help the little grin that tugged at the corners of her mouth. "And just what might that be?"

"I'll have to think about that one." He gave her a sly wink. "I don't want to make any hasty decisions."

She saw the sparkle in his eyes and a heated look that said a lot more than just hello—a look that sent a surge of earthy desire rushing through her body. He cocked his head and stared at her for a moment, a very unnerving experience that quickly brought her back to earth. She was no good at flirting and playing teasing little games, and knew she was way out of her league. She never should have tried it with him.

"Was mystery what you were trying for?"

She furrowed her brow in confusion and tilted her head to one side. "What?"

"You asked me if I thought the sunglasses gave you an air of mystery. Is that what you were trying for?"

She glanced at the ground as the embarrassment tried

to take control and felt the heat spread across her cheeks. "No, it wasn't." She looked up at him again. Rather than making fun of her, he seemed more interested in what her answer might be. "I'm sorry. I didn't mean to sound flippant. I guess I'm just not very good at this type of conversation."

He reached out and touched his fingertips to her cheek, allowing his hand to linger for a moment before withdrawing it. His voice dropped to a soft level that wrapped her in a cloak of intimacy. "What type of conversation are you good at?"

Little trails of heat followed in the wake of his touch. She had to force the words that came out as not much more than a whisper. "I only meant that I don't do very well with casual, flirty conversations. I never know what to say and usually end up feeling foolish." Her own words shocked her. She could not imagine what had prompted her to say something so personal to this complete stranger.

"I guess that brings us back full circle to my original observation that I haven't seen you around here before." He blatantly looked her up and down, sending a second tremor of excitement coursing through her veins. He reestablished eye contact, which included another quick wink. "And believe me, I would have noticed you. Did you just arrive?"

"Uh…yes. I just got off the shuttle from the airport." She waved her hand in the direction of the driveway, indicating the van parked in front of the registration lobby. She noticed the hint of confusion followed by the look of surprise that darted across his face as he shifted his attention in that direction.

His words were slightly distracted, as if he were thinking out loud rather than talking to her. "Looks like Herb made good time from the airport. He's here a little sooner than I expected.'' Then his gaze returned to her along with his devastatingly sexy smile. ''As much as I'd love to stand here and talk to you for the rest of the morning, I'm afraid I need to get to work.''

''You mean riding that bucking horse and getting thrown to the ground wasn't work? It sure looked like work to me.''

''That?'' He gave a quick glance over his shoulder toward the horse being herded out of the corral. ''No, that wasn't work. I was handling a little problem. No big deal.'' His gaze wandered toward the shuttle van again. ''I really need to be on my way.'' He climbed over the fence, then paused as he smoothed back his glossy hair and settled his hat firmly on his head. He smiled at her while touching his hand to his hat brim. ''I'll *definitely* see you later.'' He had spoken the words as a statement of fact rather than a casual comment.

She returned his smile. ''I'll look forward to it.'' Unsettled, she felt a flutter in the pit of her stomach as she watched him walk away, his stride purposeful and determined. Yes…she would like that very much in spite of the fact that he had left her feeling off balance. She knew she had just fallen instantly in lust with the sexiest man she had ever met, but there seemed to be more to it than that. He had literally rocked her senses to the core and knocked her for a loop. She toyed with the notion of love at first sight. Was there such a thing, and if so, how could someone clearly identify it? Whatever the answers, this cowboy had totally captivated her.

She turned her attention back to the shuttle van and to the reality of her objective. The driver had gotten a cart and loaded the baggage onto it. She hurried to rejoin the others, her insides still quivering from her encounter with the brash cowboy. A moment later, she spotted the same drop-dead gorgeous man headed toward the van. He smiled at her…at least it seemed that it had been directed solely for her benefit, rather than extended to the group. Or perhaps it was merely wishful thinking on her part.

He joined the new arrivals. "Good morning, ladies and gentlemen. If you'll give me a moment or two, I'll be right with you." He turned toward the driver and held out his hand. "Do you have a copy of the guest list, Herb? You got here a little sooner than I expected and caught me unprepared. Then I got sidetracked—" he shot a quick sideways glance at Lexi along with a knowing grin "—and didn't have a chance to grab the clipboard from the office."

As if to confirm his statement he brushed some dirt from his shirt and took another swipe at his jeans. A sheepish grin appeared and a hint of embarrassment darted across his features, giving him the appearance of a mischievous little boy who had just been caught with his hand in the cookie jar.

"I obviously didn't have an opportunity to get cleaned up, either."

The driver handed him a sheet of paper, then returned to the task of wheeling the baggage cart into the building.

The cowboy turned toward the group with an engaging smile. "I'm Nick Clayton. On behalf of my mother, Gloria, and my brother, Danny, I'd like to officially welcome you to the Via Verde Dude Ranch. We hope to make your vacation a fun and memorable experience."

A solid jab of alarm shot through Lexi, then it settled in the pit of her stomach where it continued to churn. A hard knot lodged in her throat as the shock jolted her senses. She tried to swallow it away, but it almost choked her. Had she heard him correctly? This sexy cowboy who had totally grabbed her attention and triggered such sensual thoughts and desires in her imagination was Nick Clayton? This man whose mere presence had sent tingles of excitement through her body and turned her world upside down was the very man she had come to confront—the man who had ruined her sister's life?

She tried to shove the contradictory clouds of confusion from her mind. On one hand, there was her steadfast belief in her need to do everything she could to secure her nephew's future, but on the other hand was her knowledge of Marnie's history of lies and deceit. It was that nagging little doubt in the back of her mind that had prompted her plan to check out Nick Clayton in person without his knowing it before taking any further action.

She forced her attention back to what he was saying.

"...you have any questions or need any assistance, please feel free to contact me or any of the staff." Nick glanced at the list in his hand. "And now, I'd like to attach some names to your faces."

He quickly identified the other people who had arrived on the shuttle van with Lexi, offering each a warm handshake of welcome. Then he turned his attention toward her and held out his hand. His voice lowered to a timbre that mesmerized her senses, nearly obliterating her determination to ignore him.

"It seems the only name left on my list is Alexandra Parker from Chicago." He grasped her hand firmly, a physical contact that lingered a couple of seconds longer than it should have as the warmth of his touch suffused her with a very real desire for more.

Again she forced away the totally inappropriate feelings caused by the nearness of this very enticing man. She attempted to dismiss them as being ridiculous. It was a purely physical attraction to a sexy man, nothing more. She was a mature adult who could put aside such unimportant nonsense and concentrate on what needed to be done.

She stared at him through narrowing eyes as she forced her mind beyond what she saw and felt to exactly who and what he was. She knew his type all too well. She had once been engaged to someone just like him—a man with a smooth technique, a fast line and not a sincere bone in his body. She had been fully prepared to hate Nick Clayton on sight.

His warm touch and the almost overwhelming pull on her senses again edged into her consciousness as she tried valiantly to get the upper hand in her internal battle. She made every effort to shove the unwelcome sensations away, but as the familiar poem said, "The best laid schemes o' mice and men…"

The sound of his voice interrupted her thoughts and jolted her back to the fact that he was talking to her.

"Is that correct? You're Alexandra Parker?"

She finally collected her wits and managed to stammer a few words. "Yes…Lexi for short…Lexi Parker."

The unexpected excitement caused by the brief moment of physical contact when they shook hands and the flash of his dazzling smile sent a shiver of sweet anticipation through her body, followed by a sobering dash of trepidation. There was no question that he was the most handsome man she had ever met, a man who oozed sex appeal by the bucketful and could probably charm a snake out of its skin—or a woman out of her good intentions, not to mention her clothes. It was easy to see how her sister could have fallen under the spell of this far too sexy cowboy even though he was not at all what Lexi had expected to find.

She felt a twinge of anger, which she immediately attributed to the fact that reality had refused to coincide with her preconceived notions. She had spent a lot of time, energy and effort planning this. She knew what she wanted to feel and what she had expected to find, but that was not what had happened when she came face-to-face with Nick Clayton. She again extended a hard glance toward him as she tried to figure out what her next step should be.

He flashed his best smile at her, covering whatever thoughts may have been running through his mind in the process. He made a notation on the list of names. ''Then Lexi it is.''

When he had first spotted her at the corral fence, all he could see was long blond hair and a great pair of tanned legs extending from cutoff jeans. As he got closer, he saw a woman with delectable curves in all the right places. When he finally came face-to-face with her and had removed her sunglasses, he discovered a beautiful woman with large hazel eyes surrounded by long, dark lashes. Her flawless skin had the appearance of smooth silk—what his mother would have referred to as a peaches-and-cream complexion.

A tightness pulled across his chest, a physical indication of just how swiftly she had reached out to him and grabbed hold of his senses. In fact, he had never had a woman make his pulse jump and his blood race that hard at first glance. He took in a deep, slow breath in an attempt to quell the feeling. This was one woman he wanted to get to know better…a whole lot better.

Then suddenly, her entire demeanor changed. She stared at him through narrowing eyes. A frown wrinkled her forehead. It was almost as if she were issuing a challenge of some sort, perhaps daring him to remember where they might have encountered each other in the past. Could she have been a guest at the ranch at some previous time? He didn't think so. He was sure he wouldn't have forgotten such a beautiful woman, but there was one way to find out.

Nick looked over the group. "Do we have any repeat guests with us today?" He again scanned the people surrounding him, his gaze settling on Lexi as she spoke up.

"My sister was a guest here a little over six years ago. Her name is Marnie Adams. Do you remember her?" She cocked her head and leveled a steady gaze at him as if she had issued a challenge and was waiting for his response.

Nick paused for a moment of concentration as he tried to recall the name, then slowly shook his head. "No...I'm sorry. The name doesn't ring a bell. You said about six years ago?" He continued to shake his head as he tried again to force some sort of recognition of the name.

"Well, it was quite a while ago. I suppose it's understandable that you wouldn't remember her."

He caught the hint of a hard edge to her voice that conveyed something quite different from her words. In direct contrast to his earlier conversation with her at the corral, she now didn't seem to fit in with the other guests. They were all happy, laughing and looking forward to their vacations. She behaved more like someone with an entirely separate agenda rather than someone anticipating a fun-filled time. And the way she looked at him—almost as if he were supposed to know who she was. A perplexing situation, but it didn't stop him from finding her to be a very intriguing and incredibly desirable woman—a thought reinforced by the tightness that continued to pull across his chest and the heat that settled low in his body.

He hadn't noticed any antagonism when they were talking at the corral, so why now? He decided to dismiss the puzzling situation as just one of those things. Perhaps she was tired from her trip or maybe he had read something into it that wasn't there. Either way, there was nothing to be gained by giving it any additional thought when there were so many more appetizing things about this woman to occupy his attention. He turned back to the business at hand.

"Herb has your luggage at the front desk. Please step inside and register. You'll find daily schedules in your rooms to help guide you in your selection of activities." He flashed his patented smile. "Once again, if there's anything you need, please don't hesitate to ask any of the staff."

His smile faded as he returned to thoughts of Lexi Parker and what was really going on in her mind. Had he unintentionally done something to offend her? He replayed their conversation at the corral in his mind, but he couldn't find anything that was okay then but would have caused her to have such a sudden change of attitude ten minutes later. She had said that she had been a little uncomfortable with the nature of a flirty conversation, but she hadn't seemed angered by it. Could he have inadvertently embarrassed her? He scanned the group as they headed toward the building, his gaze lingering on Lexi for a moment longer.

She paused on her way to the registration lobby and gave a quick glance in his direction, noting the look of puzzlement on his face, then moved along with the rest of the guests. A twinge of anger jabbed at her as she recalled his blatant denial that he even knew Marnie. She almost turned back to confront him about it, then thought better of it. She was anxious to get to her cabin so she could reevaluate the situation—and get far away from the all-too-alluring presence of Nick Clayton. This strange turn of events had totally unnerved her. So far, things hadn't gone quite as she had planned.

When Lexi made her reservation, she had requested a cabin rather than a room in the main lodge, preferring to be away from the central hub of activity. This was not a vacation as far as she was concerned. It was business— very serious business.

She registered, then went to her assigned cabin consisting of a large bedroom, a bathroom and a patio. The furnishings looked comfortable, accentuated by an attractive and tasteful decor. As advertised, there were no televisions, radios or telephones in the guests' rooms although there was a comfortable lounge in the main building with a big-screen television.

As soon as she had unpacked and put her things away, she picked up the activities schedule. She glanced at it but put it back on the table without giving it too much thought. She would make her selections later, ensuring that she participated in all the activities led by Nick Clayton. Right now, however, she had more important things on her mind.

She had formulated a plan, actually several plans, on how she would handle the situation once she arrived at the ranch. She knew it was going to take every bit of intestinal fortitude she could muster to keep her long-suppressed feelings of resentment and her hidden agenda from showing. She tried to dismiss the fact that she now needed to add the necessity of ignoring a very primal attraction to an incredibly sexy and appealing man—a man whose touch and smile made her pulse race, a man about whom she could easily fantasize making passionate love all night long...and a man she *knew* was a no-good philanderer.

At least she thought she knew it. Even though she disliked the notion, she couldn't stop thinking she'd need to confirm Marnie's story before taking any action. Before she made her move, she'd have to scope out the situation, learn as much as she could about Nick Clayton and figure out what made him tick. A touch of sadness worked its way into her mind. Even though she loved her older sister, she could not turn a blind eye to Marnie's history of twisting and exaggerating facts to suit her needs.

She could not imagine why Marnie would lie about something this important, but Lexi wanted to make sure everything had happened just as her sister said it had before she confronted Nick Clayton about his son. She didn't want to make any mistakes that would allow him an avenue of escape, nor did she want to tip her hand too soon.

She took a steadying breath and shoved away the unsettled anxiety in her stomach. But try as she might, she could not dislodge the image that continued to tempt her stimulated senses and heated desires. There was something very special about Nick Clayton that had grabbed hold of her and refused to let go.

There was no doubt that he had made a definite impact on her, but it was one she feared could end up causing an emotional upheaval in her life. From the moment she'd laid eyes on this delicious cowboy, sensual desires had dominated her thoughts—desires tempered by a softer underscoring of emotion. A link of some sort had been forged, one as much emotional as physical. She didn't understand it, but she instinctively knew it was true.

How could she possibly give her full attention to achieving her goal when the object of her quest kept heating her senses and turning her life upside down? She had never met anyone who had gotten under her skin the way he had. Her earlier errant thought about love at first sight

came back to haunt her. She had only meant it as a joke—
at least she had thought it was only a joke. Could there
have been more truth to it than she realized?

Lexi's brow furrowed in confusion as she tried to force
her thoughts and feelings into some sort of sensible and
rational mold—something that would remove them from
the influence of her emotions. A little shiver of trepidation
pricked at her consciousness. He would not be that easy
to dismiss from her life on either a physical or an emotional level.

Nick Clayton had turned out to be a very disconcerting
man. Finding out his secrets and digging into his psyche
was going to be much more difficult than she'd originally
thought.

Two

Nick entered the ranch's business office and perched on the edge of his mother's desk. "Well, what's on the agenda for the rest of today?" He picked up the clipboard, giving the schedule a quick glance. "Any problems that I need to know about?"

Gloria Clayton looked up at her older son, emitted a little sigh of resignation and took the clipboard away from him. "Nothing out of the ordinary that can't be handled as part of the daily routine by the people whose job it is." She released the brake on her wheelchair and started across the room.

Nick jumped to his feet. "What do you need? I'll get it for you."

Gloria wheeled around to face him. "Nicky...I've been confined to this chair for a little over eight years now. I've adjusted to your father being gone and I've adjusted to not being able to walk more than a few steps unaided.

I'm more than capable of getting whatever I need by myself.''

A moment of sorrow swept across her features and her words came out barely above a whisper. ''One moment, a blink of an eye, and the entire world is turned upside down. Your father is dead, my legs are almost useless, and the drunk driver who ran the red light and crashed into our car walks away without a scratch.''

She looked up at her son, a gentle smile coming to her still-beautiful features. ''And out of that terrible happening came a new beginning. A modest cattle ranch becomes a successful dude ranch. You and Danny stepped into your father's shoes and did a terrific job of making the difficult transition and running the business.'' The gentle smile turned to an amused chuckle. ''Now, if I could just get you to stop trying to be all things to everyone and start thinking about yourself for a change.'' A pensive look crossed her face. ''There must be some kind of a middle ground between your serious approach to responsibility and Danny's frivolous, good-time attitude.''

''Ah—Danny's frivolous, good-time attitude.'' He nervously shifted his weight and cleared his throat. ''Well, maybe he'll grow up one of these days.''

''He's twenty-eight years old, Nicky. And you're thirty. Neither of you are children anymore.''

Nick carefully sidestepped Gloria's comments about what she had often referred to as his overinflated sense of responsibility, preferring to allow Danny to be the topic of conversation. ''There is one thing Danny does that I'm happy to let him handle without any interference. He works real well with the kids. I…uh…'' One of Nick's very few chinks in his armor of confidence was now visible. ''I haven't a clue what to do with children. I sort of freeze up when I'm around them and am at a loss for something to say. I guess I just don't know how to talk to kids.''

''Well, one of these days you'll come face-to-face with the perfect woman and that will be the end of your objections. You'll look up and there she'll be. You'll get married and have a family of your own. I remember when your father and I met. One look and we both knew that was it.'' Gloria shot him a half teasing, half serious glance. ''One of these days I'll finally be a grandmother. I'm the only one of all my friends who doesn't have any grandchildren.''

Nick chuckled nervously. ''Now, Mom. There's plenty of time for that.'' He placed a loving kiss on her forehead and grinned at her. ''You're far too young to be a grandmother.''

He felt the tension building inside him. It was a conversation that always made him uneasy. He really had no interest in getting married. He had a business to run and too many people depended on him for their jobs, a responsibility that took most of his time and weighed heavily on his shoulders. There was no way he would be able to take on the additional commitment that marriage required. Besides, why tie himself down to only one woman when there were so many out there to choose from?

He and Danny had both found that the unmarried female guests at their dude ranch provided a perfect short-term, no-strings-attached type of relationship. They arrived in groups of two or three and quickly made their availability known. As ranch guests they were there to have a good time and forget about the problems of everyday life. No one was looking for anything serious. It lasted for two or three weeks, everyone enjoyed themselves, then the guests returned to their homes and new guests arrived.

Danny flirted outrageously while Nick was more selective and usually more discreet, but each had no problem attracting feminine companionship. Danny called it the best of all possible worlds.

It always made Nick uncomfortable when his mother started talking about grandchildren, which meant she was really talking about his getting married. That was one responsibility he was definitely not ready to accept. And then, as if on cue, an image of Lexi Parker's face popped into his mind...again. It was a situation that had repeated itself at least ten times in the past couple of hours.

There was no denying the fact that she had assaulted his senses in a way no other woman ever had. Everything about her...the shapely tanned legs, the way the soft fabric of her blouse caressed the curve of her breasts, the tilt of her head, the intelligence in her beautiful hazel eyes, her flawless skin, a throaty voice that sent tremors of longing through his body, a perfect mouth that absolutely begged to be kissed—

His mother's voice intruded into his errant thoughts. "Isn't it at about this point in the conversation when you decide you have some very urgent business that slipped your mind and then you hurry out of here?" There may have been teasing in her voice, but there was seriousness in her eyes.

The interruption was a welcome one, especially considering where those tempting images were taking him. He began to edge toward the door as he flashed his best "trust me" smile. "I don't know where you get these crazy ideas." He glanced at his watch. "Uh-oh. I didn't realize it was so late. I have some paperwork to take care of."

Nick headed down the hall, Lexi Parker continuing to

invade his thoughts and linger in his mind. He had even gone so far as to check her reservation information. He knew she had arrived alone, but she had also requested a single cabin, which told him she was not expecting anyone to join her. He thought back to her mention of her sister, someone who had been a previous guest at the ranch. Why would she come alone rather than with a friend or even her sister? It piqued his curiosity, but then everything about Lexi Parker piqued his curiosity as well as heated his desires.

It had been quite a while since a woman made his blood race that hard and fast at first glance. He closed his eyes for a moment as he recalled the surge of electricity from her touch when they shook hands. This was definitely a woman he wanted to know—*intimately* know—as quickly as possible. Thoughts of Lexi Parker did more than just pique Nick's curiosity. He could picture her long blond hair spread out across his pillow and that incredibly tempting mouth beckoning him to partake.

As he passed the door leading into the lobby he spotted Lexi entering from the front of the building. She crossed the lobby toward the registration desk. He quickly stepped through the door to intercept her.

"Hello, Lexi." He felt his breath quicken and his pulse begin to race. He flashed a sexy grin as he leaned against the counter, trying to appear casual even though it was far removed from the unsettled feeling that had a grip on him. "Are you getting situated okay? Is there anything I can help you with?"

"I was just turning in my activities sign-up sheet."

"I'll be happy to take care of that for you." He took the sheet of paper from her and glanced over her selections. He managed to maintain an outer calm despite the way her nearness pulled on his senses and desires. She exerted a very disconcerting effect on him. He wanted to pull her into his arms, claim her delicious-looking mouth as his and whisk her away to his cabin for an afternoon of totally uninhibited passion.

He looked up, locking eye contact with her for a second before allowing his gaze to momentarily drop to the temptation of her slightly parted lips. "This is quite an energetic schedule you've set for yourself. Most of our guests like to kick back and relax for the first couple of days before throwing themselves into the more rigorous activities."

He glanced at her list again. "I see you're starting out first thing in the morning with our sunrise breakfast ride. In fact, you've signed up for it twice this week." He arched one eyebrow in surprise. "And you're going to try our calf-roping lessons in preparation for the guest rodeo?" He looked up at her, catching a fleeting glimpse of uncertainty in her eyes that quickly changed to something more standoffish. "We don't have too many women who try their hand at calf roping. You must be quite the outdoors enthusiast."

"Uh…well, yes. I do enjoy being outdoors." Every activity led by Nick Clayton had gone on her sign-up sheet. She had to know more about him to determine the best way to confront him about his son—well, at least determine if Jimmy was his son. *If* Jimmy was his son? How had she allowed that doubt to become part of her thinking? She stiffened her resolve and tried to shove the uncertainties aside. She had to see this through to the conclusion.

But *calf roping?* A hint of trepidation shivered up her back. Did she really need to go that far? The last time she was on a horse had been during her freshman year of college. Things seemed to be turning into an endurance test and she wasn't sure she had the stamina to last the entire three weeks. A groan tried to claw its way out of her throat. She hoped she would be able to physically survive the implementation of her plan.

The worst part was the nagging feeling that she had not signed up for all of Nick's activities strictly to fulfill the task she had set for herself—that perhaps there was a more personal motive behind it. She was incredibly attracted to Nick Clayton and didn't seem to have any control over it. It was more than just his sexy smile and handsome features. There was a strength about him, a confidence that reached out and touched her on a deeply emotional level.

A bit of a smile turned the corners of Lexi's mouth as she slowly regained her composure and rallied a new determination. "I thought I'd go swimming this afternoon, soak up some sunshine and enjoy this beautiful scenery while breathing your nice, clean air." She would show him that he could not work his charm on her that easily. It would take more than a handsome cowboy in a pair of tight jeans to turn her head and make her abandon her plans.

Was it false confidence on her part? Again, she was not sure exactly which part of her was in charge—the woman who was ready to fight tooth and nail to get little Jimmy what he rightly deserved or the woman who had never met anyone like Nick Clayton and hadn't a clue how to break the spell he seemed to be casting over her.

She clenched her jaw in resolve. It had better be the first woman who was in charge because that other one didn't stand a chance against this charming scoundrel.

Nick leaned slightly forward and lowered his voice to a sensual tone conveying the feeling that his words were meant for her ears only even though no one else was within earshot. "It appears that we'll be spending a lot of time together since I'm in charge of the activities you've listed on your sheet."

He extended a warm smile, very pleased at this interesting turn of events. It was as if fate had literally dropped her into his lap. It couldn't have worked out better if she had purposely intended to spend as much time with him as possible—a prospect that sent a ripple of hope through his body and heightened his already heated desires. He reached out and brushed a wayward tendril of hair away from her cheek, allowing his fingertips to linger against her skin for a couple of seconds.

Then, as if his hand had a will of its own, he cupped her chin in his palm. He hesitated a moment, then leaned forward, bringing his face very close to hers until their lips were only a heartbeat apart. He could feel her breathing and almost taste her sweetness. Then he felt her body stiffen and the magic of the moment disintegrated.

She took a step backward from his electrifying touch as she cleared her throat of the sensation that her heart had lodged there. Perhaps he didn't see their accidental meeting as a sparring match, but she did. And so far, the intense attraction she felt toward him had kept her almost tongue-tied and incapable of thinking clearly. The very last thing she wanted was to acknowledge the fact that she had almost allowed him to kiss her.

She noted the way he raised a questioning eyebrow, but he didn't say anything. She needed to regain the upper hand. She held her breath for a brief moment in order to recapture her composure, then plunged ahead. "I was wondering if you'd had an opportunity to give any more thought to my sister...maybe recall her staying here. She spoke so highly of those two weeks that I decided to spend my vacation here."

To her surprise, he straightened up and appeared to be trying to collect himself. Had she hit a nerve? A touch of satisfaction tickled her consciousness. Maybe this would be easier than she had thought. If she could take care of her objective very quickly, then she could return to her own home. She felt decidedly unsafe—*emotionally* at risk—around this disconcerting man. Nick Clayton frightened her. The very real attraction she felt toward him frightened her. She feared she might be incapable of denying him whatever he asked of her.

"Well, no...actually, I haven't had the time. You said her name was Marnie Adams? The name does have a familiar ring to it now that I'm thinking about it, but I'm afraid I still can't place her. Perhaps it will come to me after I've had the chance to give it some thought."

"Yes, perhaps it will." She heard the edge to her voice and silently berated herself for allowing it to seep through.

"That's kind of odd."

"What's odd?" Had she missed something? It was as if he had changed topics on her while she wasn't listening.

"You said your sister was here a little over six years ago, loved her stay, spoke of it in glowing terms, which prompted you to take your vacation here."

"Yes...what's so odd about that?"

"I was just wondering why you waited six years."

His words caught her totally off guard. It hadn't occurred to her to develop a cover story, at least not anything other than what she had already given him. She frantically searched her mind for an acceptable response to his question.

"Well...uh...you know. It was just one of those things. First there was the money, then something came up and...well, you know how that goes."

"Sure, things happen." He ran his fingertips across the

back of her hand and offered his best smile. "I'm glad you were finally able to work it out."

She eased her hand out from under his as she tried to still the tremor of excitement caused by his touch. Even after she had pulled her hand free, she could still feel the warmth of his skin against hers. His smile and his words may have said he accepted her answer, but she could see it in his eyes...the questions, the skepticism, the reserve that said he didn't believe her. She scanned the lobby in an attempt to find something that would let her gracefully extract herself from the conversation.

When she couldn't find anything, she returned her attention to Nick and gave him a pleasant smile. "I'm sure you have a lot to do so I won't take up any more of your time." She turned and left the lobby through the front door, forcing herself to proceed casually even though she could feel his eyes on her...and the tingle of excitement it caused.

Nick leaned back against the wall as he watched her walk away, his heart pounding and his pulse throbbing in time with each step she took. His gaze traced every line and curve of her body. When she finally disappeared through the front door, he closed his eyes and emitted a soft moan that came out as half desire and half frustration.

He took a calming breath, then decided to look into the matter of Lexi's sister. For some reason, it seemed important to her that he remember Marnie Adams and her stay at the ranch. Rather than go to his office, he made a side trip to the storage room. Six years ago—he searched for the corresponding storage boxes. Time was forgotten as he immersed himself in the task.

"Aha!" The sound of his own voice echoing through the quiet startled him. There it was—Marnie Adams.

He opened the file and quickly scanned the contents,

then went back and carefully reread everything. A slight furrow wrinkled his brow as he checked her original reservation and her registration card. She had vacationed alone, too. First Marnie, then her sister, vacationing alone at a dude ranch. Very curious...very curious indeed. He checked Marnie's activity sheet. Unlike Lexi, Marnie had not been involved in any strenuous pastimes. In fact, the records indicated she had not been on a horse during her entire stay.

He went to the candid publicity pictures they'd shot during that month and carefully checked the names of those who had been captured on film. He found her name and pulled the photo, one taken at a chuck-wagon barbecue.

The image shot off the paper at him. Marnie Adams bore a striking family resemblance to Lexi, making it clear that the two women were related. He studied the photograph for a few seconds. Where Lexi's look was softly sensual and *very* enticing, Marnie had a hard edge to her appearance as if she had seen too much of the world and found it a great disappointment.

Seeing the photograph jarred his memory. Marnie Adams...she had told him more about herself than he ever wanted to know. Even though she had only been in her mid-twenties at the time, she had talked about having two ex-husbands and a string of casual affairs. It was almost as if she had been bragging about those things, thinking it somehow made her seem worldly and sophisticated, the truth being quite the opposite. Even though Marnie was an undeniably beautiful woman, she had not struck a responsive chord with him.

Marnie had presented herself at his cabin door late one night with a bottle of wine in her hand. A moment later, she revealed that she had nothing on beneath her robe. He tactfully, but firmly, refused her offer and sent her on her way. The blatant invitation had been tempting, but she was obviously drunk. Other men might have considered that type of situation as easy pickings, but that certainly wasn't his style.

The next morning, she acted as if the incident had never happened. He acknowledged that due to her inebriated condition she might not have even remembered what she'd done. When he made love with a woman, he wanted it to damn well be something they would both enjoy and remember the next morning.

That had been a little over six years ago. So, what was Marnie's sister doing at the ranch now and why did he feel that something was wrong? Was it just his imagination or was there more to it than that? There was no question that he felt a very strong physical attraction to Lexi, an attraction he fully intended to pursue. It was something that most certainly had not existed with Marnie.

He closed his eyes for a moment and allowed a smile to curl the corners of his mouth as he entertained a totally inappropriate thought. Well, maybe not inappropriate, but probably unlikely. He visualized Lexi Parker presenting herself at his door, carrying a bottle of wine and wearing nothing but a—

"There you are!" Danny Clayton's irritation interrupted Nick's errant musings.

Nick whirled around to face the six-foot-tall man with the sandy-colored hair. "And where should I be?" He arched one eyebrow and leveled a serious gaze at his brother as much in an attempt to cover his embarrassment at being caught daydreaming as anything else.

Danny glanced at his watch. "In five minutes you're supposed to be at the corral—" he grinned and slipped into an exaggerated slow drawl while doing his best John

Wayne impersonation ''—to saddle 'em up, pilgrim, and move 'em on out for the afternoon ride.'' He stepped into the storeroom and looked around. ''So, what are you doing in here?''

Nick attempted to sound casual as if nothing out of the ordinary had been going on. ''I was checking on a guest who stayed here a few years ago. Her sister arrived this morning and mentioned it.'' He handed the photograph to Danny and indicated Marnie. ''Do you remember her?''

Danny took the photograph from Nick and studied it for a moment. ''Oh, yeah. I remember this one all right. She was one hot little number.''

Nick stared at his brother, not sure exactly how to interpret what Danny said. ''Oh? Do I take that to mean that you—''

''No, not me. I just meant that she seemed to be really hot for cowboys and was determined to get it on with as many as possible. I made it a point to stay clear of her.'' A wicked little grin tugged at his lips. ''She seemed to be more interested in quantity than quality.''

Nick returned the photograph to the file, stuck the file folder into the storage box and shoved it aside with the toe of his boot.

Danny shot Nick a knowing look. ''Well, well, well…the sister who's the newly arrived guest wouldn't be that tasty-looking blonde you've been drooling over ever since the shuttle van arrived from the airport, would it?''

Nick hid behind a stern expression. ''Knock it off, Danny. I haven't been *drooling* over anyone.'' He attempted to project a businesslike manner. ''Lexi simply mentioned that her sister had vacationed here a few years ago and asked if I remembered meeting her. I was just looking through the old records to see if I could find a photograph to jog my memory. It's no big deal."

"Oh, I see." Danny could no longer suppress a mischievous grin. "Then I can assume you have no personal interest in Ms. Lexi Parker? That you don't have any objections to my making a play for her?"

Nick balled up his fist, gave his brother a loving punch to the shoulder, then broke out into a teasing smile. "You do and you die!"

Danny returned the feeling of closeness between the brothers. "That's what I thought."

Lexi forced a smile and tried to assume an upbeat manner as she stepped into the dining room. She turned to the attractive gray-haired woman seated at the front desk.

"Lexi Parker...one for dinner."

The older woman extended her hand toward Lexi and offered a gracious smile. "I'm Gloria Clayton. It's a pleasure to meet you, Lexi."

"Thank you. It's nice to meet you, Gloria."

"On behalf of my two sons and myself, I'd like to thank you for choosing to spend your vacation with us. The weather forecast says blue skies and sunshine for the next few days, so there won't be anything standing in the way of your having a great time."

Lexi could see the family resemblance between Nick and his mother. She was a charming woman who exuded warmth and sincerity. Lexi instantly liked her. "I'm sure I will. The scenery here is truly spectacular, and coming from a large city, I can assure you that I'm really enjoying all this clean mountain air."

Gloria smiled. "It's good for flagging appetites, too. Now, about the meals. They're all served family style. That gives the guests an additional opportunity to get to know each other. So if you'll just follow me, I'll show you to your table.''

Gloria wheeled out from behind the desk and headed across the room. Lexi had not realized until that moment that Gloria was in a wheelchair.

Gloria showed her to a round table set with ten places. Not more than five minutes passed before nine of the ten places at her table were filled. She glanced around the dining room, noting that it was quickly filling with ranch guests. A festive mood prevailed with everyone enjoying themselves. She spotted Gloria seated at another table and a man she assumed to be Danny Clayton at yet another. A minute later, someone sat down in the chair next to hers. She turned toward the new arrival and found herself staring into Nick Clayton's blue eyes.

"Good evening, Lexi. I hope you're hungry. I just took a quick tour through the kitchen and everything looks good.''

She forced a smile. "Yes, it certainly smells good.'' Nick Clayton…was there no way to avoid constant contact with him? It seemed that every time she left her cabin she ran into him. Her purpose in being at the ranch had been to confront him. Except now she wished she could stay away from his very disconcerting presence. He made her feel uncomfortable, arousing totally inappropriate longings and desires. She wasn't sure which disturbed her more—how he made her feel or the implication of those feelings.

To her surprise, dinner turned out to be a much more pleasant interlude than she had anticipated. She was very conscious about her choice of words and tone of voice. She would occasionally slip and her conversation with Nick would border on adversarial, but only for a moment. She quickly brought it back to neutral. She reluctantly had to admit that he was a gracious host for the table. He managed to engage everyone in conversation and made sure all the guests were put at ease and felt a part of the group. She was surprised to find that he was very intelligent and conversant on a wide variety of topics. There was a lot more to this cowboy than a set of broad shoulders, a killer smile and brilliant blue eyes.

Lexi found it very unsettling. She had almost convinced herself that she would be able to ignore her unexpected yet very real attraction to him—almost. She still had not been able to set aside the threat of emotional upheaval every time he came near her. And now that she had seen that he was something other than just another libido-driven and self-absorbed handsome hunk, she did not know what to think.

A moment later, he jolted her once again.

Three

"**I** went back through the old files this afternoon and found a photograph of your sister taken at one of the barbecues. As soon as I saw her picture, it jogged my memory." Nick saw a hint of something that looked like vindication dart through Lexi's eyes, but he didn't understand where it had come from.

"Oh? So you remember her now?"

He caught her tone of voice. There it was again, that feeling of being hit with a challenge of some sort. He certainly had no intention of telling her about her sister's unseemly behavior. He wasn't sure what to say. "I can see a definite family resemblance between you and your sister."

Nick had not offered any further comment about Marnie and Lexi decided not to ask. For the time being, it was enough of a victory that he admitted knowing her.

The rest would come later. She would take it one step at a time.

Most of the other people at Lexi's table had left following dessert. Some had mentioned dropping by next door to the Hoedown Saloon for some dancing, while others had said they were going to take a walk to exercise off dinner.

Nick leaned over to her as he draped his arm across the back of her chair. He dropped his voice to a soft near whisper that sent little ripples of titillation across her skin. "Could I entice you to join me at the saloon for a dance, or maybe an after-dinner drink?"

"I...I think I'll just take a walk to settle some of this delicious dinner. I overindulged and feel the need of a little exercise and fresh air. I'm also rather tired. It's been a long day. I think I'll just turn in after my walk."

"That sounds like an excellent idea. I'll show you around the grounds. It's a beautiful night and the sky is filled with millions of brilliant stars—a perfect time for a stroll." He rose from his chair and held out his hand to assist her, proceeding as if she had agreed to his offer without giving her a chance to say no.

Lexi hesitated, torn between what she knew she should do and what she wanted to do. Then, as if he had usurped her will, she placed her hand in his. The moment they came into physical contact, a potent charge of heated desire, closely followed by an emotional tug, invaded her consciousness. She knew at once it had been a terrible mistake, but it was too late. Once again, the magnetic draw of his masculinity reeled in her senses like a fish caught on a line and she seemed helpless to prevent it.

He escorted her outside, gently guiding her with a hand at the small of her back. They strolled along a path through a stand of fir trees, then around the edge of a large reflecting pond. The brilliance of the star-filled sky, the crisp smell of the night air and the intoxicating nearness of Nick Clayton all combined to work their magic on her. The conversation was equally soft and intimate.

"Tell me about yourself, about your family. I know you have a sister. Do you have any brothers?"

She tried to give him as little information as possible without arousing his suspicions. "No brothers, just my sister and me. My father died ten years ago and my mother lives in Chicago, as I do."

"Are you originally from Chicago?"

"Yep…born and raised. I went away to college but returned after graduation and have worked there ever since."

"What do you do for a living?"

A feeling of discomfort stabbed at her. This was all wrong. She was supposed to be finding out about him, not the other way around. He had moved her along so smoothly that she had barely been aware of what was happening. She tried to force a laugh, as if making a joke. "You're making me feel as if I were some sort of specimen to be studied under a microscope."

A hint of an embarrassed chuckle escaped his throat. "I didn't mean to sound like I was cross-examining you on the witness stand." He grasped her hand, then stopped walking, bringing her to an abrupt halt. "I'm genuinely interested." He searched the depths of her hazel eyes. "We can talk about something else if you'd rather. What topics interest you?"

"Well—" her mind worked quickly as Lexi tried to figure a way to turn this to her advantage "—it seems to me that turnabout is fair play. So, tell me about yourself. Have you always lived here?"

"Yep…this ranch belonged to my grandfather, then my

father. When my father died, it passed on to my mother, my brother and me. It's always been a cattle ranch, but we made some changes a few years ago and turned it into a dude ranch. We still run a small cattle operation, but being a dude ranch is our main business now."

"There's just the three of you—Gloria, Danny and yourself?"

"That's right." A little grin tugged at the corners of his mouth and his eyes sparkled. "Now, what else would you like to know? I'm thirty years old, Danny is twenty-eight. I stand six-one without my boots. I have a degree in business administration from the University of Washington and Danny has one in liberal arts from Colorado State. I don't think I have a favorite color. As far as food goes, I'll eat just about anything. I enjoy fine wine, but on a hot, dusty day, a cold beer tastes real good. I read a lot and like movies—mysteries are my favorite. My musical tastes are fairly broad with a particular fondness for jazz."

"Oh, my...I'm...uh..." He had left her speechless with his sudden burst of personal information.

It had all come out so suddenly...and so honestly. Everything about him seemed so straightforward, something she found confusing. Nothing about him seemed to coincide with the type of men Marnie usually chose. Lexi's casual conversation with Nick Clayton had done nothing to help clarify what had happened between him and her sister...*if* anything had actually happened.

She cleared her throat in an attempt to drive away her doubts. "I guess it's my turn to be embarrassed. I certainly didn't mean—"

He touched his fingertips to her lips to still her words. "That's okay. No harm done."

He continued to clasp her hand as they started walking

again. She felt as if she were walking through a dream…with the man of her dreams. It was exciting and at the same time frightening. The warmth of his touch began to melt away her resistance. She hadn't anticipated this type of personal involvement, and the emotional overtones were particularly unsettling. She didn't welcome it, but neither did she seem able to turn her back and walk away. They finally arrived at her cabin.

Millions of stars sparkled like diamonds on a black velvet background, each point of light casting a spell on the moment. Nick didn't know if it was simply the magic of the night or the exhilaration caused by the nearness of a beautiful and desirable woman, but he felt himself being drawn in by more than a physical attraction and a longing to make love to her. He also wanted to know her, to discover who she was under that unpredictable exterior. At times, she seemed everything a man could ever want, then suddenly she'd become distant as if she had just remembered who she was or why she was there.

"Well, here we are. Your home sweet home for the next three weeks." He glanced at his watch. "It's still early. Could I tempt you with a glass of wine before calling it a night?"

"I don't think so." She felt as if all the oxygen had suddenly been sucked from the air. His face was so close to hers, the faint illumination highlighting his handsome features. She tried to project a casual manner as if this were nothing more than a normal end to a normal day. "I have a sunrise breakfast ride in the morning and sunrise comes very early."

"So it does." His words were more like a caress against her cheek than simply conversation.

Her throat went dry. She literally forced out her words. "And I need to get some sleep if I'm going to—"

The rest of her words were lost along with her thoughts when Nick Clayton brushed his lips against hers, then drew her into his embrace as he captured her mouth fully with a delicious and sensually heated kiss. And like a moth drawn to a flame, she could not resist regardless of the risk involved.

Her mind went blank, devoid of everything except the feel of his lips against hers, the way he had pulled her body tight against his, and the overwhelming need to have much more of this dangerous man than merely a kiss. She raised her arms until they encircled his neck.

Random thoughts tried to penetrate the sensual cloud fogging her brain. This man ruined her sister's life…this bounder wouldn't treat her any better than he had Marnie…this man was a forbidden treat glistening on the horizon, tempting, beckoning…this man was no good for her. But still she savored the excitement of his touch, the delicious truth of his kiss as he pulled her body tighter against his.

He reveled in her intoxicating taste and the feel of her body pressed along the length of his. She had the power to drive him to total distraction and she didn't even seem to be aware of it. He knew he would not be satisfied until he intimately knew every inch of her. And if the burning need surging through his body was any indication, he would still want more. He finally broke off the kiss.

His voice came out as a husky whisper. "I have an excellent bottle of wine in my cabin and a private hot tub on my enclosed patio. Could I entice you to join me?"

His words sent a tremor of nervousness through her body. He had no idea how easy it would be to entice her. In fact, it took every bit of the determination she could muster just to keep from dragging him inside her cabin, shoving him down on her bed and ripping off his clothes.

What was the matter with her? She'd never felt this way about any other man, and this was the wrong man to— She gulped in a steadying breath, then another, before she attempted to speak. She knew she needed to sound totally in control.

"It's late."

"Yes." He leaned forward and brushed his mouth lightly against her kiss-swollen lips. "I guess it is." He directed one last look of longing in her direction. "I'll see you at sunrise." With that, he turned and walked away.

Lexi quickly went inside her cabin, closed the door and leaned back against it with her eyes squeezed tightly shut. Her pounding heart raced with her ragged breathing. She touched her fingertips to her lips as she tried to catch her breath. No one had ever kissed her like that before in her entire life. She felt the heat all the way down to her toes. Even now, she felt an ache deep inside her that she knew could be soothed only by the touch of Nick Clayton.

The fantasies she had conjured up about him earlier paled in comparison with the reality of the passions of this man—this truly forbidden man. She shivered. She had to get herself under control and get back on track... somehow.

She walked into the bathroom, sat on the edge of the tub and stared at herself in the mirror. She saw the doubt that clouded her features. She didn't feel as confident about this whole thing as she had when she left Chicago. Hopefully, it was nothing more than a temporary bout of anxiety over whether she was doing the right thing in being here at all, rather than the power of this provocative man's touch and the disturbingly real effect he seemed to have on her.

She shook her head to rid herself of the unwelcome

thoughts that insisted on popping up at the most inopportune times. Maybe her mother had been right. Maybe she was too headstrong for her own good and her being at the ranch was a really stupid idea. Another shiver of trepidation made its way through her body as if to confirm the doubts that started plaguing her from the moment she learned the identity of the captivating cowboy and felt the warmth of his touch when their hands clasped.

She forced her determination to the surface. She had to pull her emotions together and tuck them away. It was too late to turn back. No matter where her unexpected attraction to Nick Clayton took her, it did not alter the fact that a little five-year-old boy deserved more than what he had. She didn't want to make any costly mistakes that would allow Nick a way out of his responsibility to his son…*if* Jimmy was, indeed, his son.

It was all very puzzling. The Via Verde was simply not Marnie's style. It was the very last place she would ever have expected to find her sister, yet she had the postcards Marnie had mailed her from the ranch. And Marnie's claim that Nick had taken her to Hawaii—she also had the postcards Marnie had sent her from Honolulu. She knew the part about Marnie's being in Hawaii was true, but she only had Marnie's word that Nick Clayton was the man who had taken her there.

Now that she knew what Nick Clayton looked like, she realized there had been no photographs in Marnie's personal effects showing Marnie and Nick together, nor even any photographs of Nick by himself. Of course, when Nick had rejected her, she could have thrown them all in the trash. But still it was very puzzling.

And now that she had found out for herself how devastatingly real his allure was, all she could do was stare at herself in the mirror and wonder what she had gotten herself into. An audible sigh escaped her throat as she rose to her feet and undressed for bed even though she knew sleep would surely elude her.

Images of Nick Clayton continued to dance through her mind. His touch...the sound of his voice...the devastatingly sexy smile...the way he made her heart pound and her senses reel...and the heat of a passionate kiss that nearly singed her lips. If she had not known who and what he was, she would have been very anxious to pursue something more with him...a *lot* more.

She clenched her jaw in a hard line of determination. All her speculation was ridiculous. He couldn't be trusted. She knew exactly who and what he was. All she needed to do was find a way to confirm her information, then confront him with the facts. She would see to it that this irresponsible playboy never forgot Marnie's name again. She shut her eyes, but she could not shut out the image of Nick Clayton or the disturbing and totally inappropriate thoughts of desire and fulfillment. Neither could she dismiss her growing concerns about what was true and what might have been Marnie's exaggerations.

Nick arrived at the stables before daylight to help with the preparations for the breakfast ride. He worked with the wranglers to match horses with riders according to their stated level of expertise on the activities form. He kept physically busy, but his thoughts were not on the work. Too many questions continued to circulate through his mind. The time he had spent with Lexi the previous evening had been as disturbing to him as it had been exciting. There was no question that she was not just another happy vacationer, but that did not tell him what she was.

He studied Lexi's sign-up sheet. She had professed some riding experience, but not a great deal of proficiency, which did not match with her having signed up for calf-roping lessons. He dismissed the thought. Perhaps she had just gotten caught up in the spirit of ranch life and simply wanted to try different things. He reflected on the information he had found on Marnie's old activities sheet showing that she had not registered for one single activity that involved anything remotely strenuous.

Twelve people had signed up for the sunrise breakfast ride that morning, including Lexi. Nick and two of his wranglers would be able to easily handle that size group. They set about saddling the horses. When that task was completed, he hurried toward the staging area at the back of the kitchen to make sure the chuck wagon was properly loaded and the cook and his helper ready to head out.

The chuck wagon would go directly to the meadow, where the two men would set up and start preparing breakfast. Nick and the wranglers would take the group of riders on a trail that ran along the river, then over to the meadow to meet up with the chuck wagon. Following breakfast, they would go on a two-hour ride, returning to the stables just before noon. He looked toward the east, to the first gray streaks of dawn. It was going to be a beautiful day for a ride.

Nick felt a little pang of anxiety as the time drew near for the guests to start gathering for the ride. He had never had anxieties about the next morning where other women were concerned. And this was only a kiss, not a night of wild sex. He couldn't explain the strange feeling, but he did know that he wasn't happy about it. He returned his attention to handling the last-minute details.

Lexi stood at her cabin window. For the past half hour she had been peering at the lighted area of the corral, watching the early-morning activity. She had been surprised to see Nick working alongside the wranglers rather than merely supervising. She paid particular attention to him, noting the way he double-checked everything. Nothing escaped his close scrutiny. His were certainly not the actions of an irresponsible man who thought only of himself.

She stiffened her resolve. He was tending to business— an entirely different matter altogether. Being conscientious about his job, especially when he owned the business, did not mean that he would be equally responsible in his personal life.

She stepped away from the window, then nervously paced across her room. Fearing she would appear too anxious, she didn't want to leave her cabin until some of the other guests had gathered at the corral. She felt a tremor of apprehension as if acknowledging her fear of being alone with him. She didn't know exactly what to say or how to act.

Was the kiss they shared just standard procedure for him? Something that would have no meaning in the bright light of day? Had he treated Marnie the same way...making her feel very special while in reality she was just another unattached female guest and temporary plaything? Lexi wasn't sure she could handle his indifference if it were just the two of them. But in a group, he would of necessity need to treat her the same as all the others.

Was it possible that he might be feeling some of the same anxiety as she was? The man who had deserted Marnie certainly wouldn't be, but was Nick Clayton really that man? She wasn't as sure about anything as she had been when she boarded the plane in Chicago. Not only had she failed to resolve any of the issues she brought with her, she now had a new one to add to the list—guilt.

She shuddered. Anxiety welled inside her. How could she have allowed him to kiss her like that? How could she have so callously betrayed her loyalty to Marnie's memory? She took a deep breath and held it for a moment, then slowly exhaled while emitting an audible sigh.

She left her cabin and headed toward the corral.

When Nick finally saw her approaching, every heated desire and libidinous thought from the night before came back full force. For the past ten minutes, every time someone approached the corral, he felt a little tingle of excitement wrap itself around him as he peered through the early-morning light, hoping to see Lexi.

He stepped forward and greeted everyone who had gathered at the corral. "Good morning, ladies and gentlemen. It's nice to see all of you at this ridiculously early hour. I hope you have your appetites with you because we have a great breakfast waiting for us in about half an hour. Now it's time to mount up. We've tried to match each rider to a horse according to your stated level of riding expertise. When I call your name, please step forward. We'll be getting under way in just a couple of minutes, but first I'd like to go over a few safety considerations."

Lexi listened carefully to each word. His efficiency and professionalism struck her above all else. He stressed safety along with having a good time. Again, there was nothing irresponsible in the way he handled things.

She went to her horse when he called her name. His voice dropped to a low level, preventing anyone else from hearing him. "It's nice to see you this morning. Did you get a good night's sleep?"

His words seemed half teasing and half serious. Was he making fun of the way she insisted on getting a good night's sleep, and in the process sending him and his passionate kisses away from her door? Then she felt his lips tickle across her cheek as he leaned forward to help her check the cinch strap on the saddle, the way he'd shown all the other guests. And once again, everything else faded into the background as her heated desires told her she wanted far more.

A few minutes later, riders and horses started along the trail. The sky went through every shade of pink and gold before turning a bright blue. The crisp morning air stimulated her senses and whetted her appetite. She kept a watchful eye on Nick. Nothing escaped his attention. The most minuscule of details failed to elude his scrutiny. One of the wranglers rode at the head of the group, which was strung out in a long line, while the other one brought up the rear. Nick and his horse seemed to move as if they were one, a perfect pairing of rider and mount. He was in constant motion up and down the line, making sure everything and everyone was okay.

As soon as they rounded a curve in the trail, the smell of frying bacon filled the air. Lexi's stomach growled in response to the tantalizing aroma. A moment later, she saw the chuck wagon in the meadow. A long table sporting a red-and-white-checkered tablecloth and folding chairs were set up next to it. The wrangler in the lead headed the group off the trail, and in a few minutes everyone dismounted. The guests quickly descended on the table, took plates and headed toward the chuck wagon.

Nick grabbed two plates and handed one of them to Lexi. "Here. I hope you're hungry."

She took it from him, their eye contact holding a second longer than necessary. She quickly glanced away as embarrassment began to take over. "I'm famished."

They filled their plates, then he escorted her to a chair and sat next to her. He maintained the same charming manner with the guests as he had at dinner the night before and was the perfect host. But that did not stop the desirous looks he directed her way or the numerous times he reached under the table and playfully ran his fingertips across the back of her hand...once even along the seam of her jeans where they stretched along the outer edge of her thigh.

Finally, Lexi shoved herself back from the table. "I'm stuffed! I can't believe I ate that much breakfast, especially after making such a pig of myself at dinner last night." She stood up and stretched her arms above her head. "It must be all this fresh mountain air."

Nick rose and gently guided her toward the chuck wagon as they continued their conversation. A moment later, they were behind the wagon and out of sight of everyone else. Nick pulled her into his embrace and whispered in her ear, "The mountain air whets the appetite for all sort of things, not the least of which is this."

He captured her mouth with a kiss far more delicious than breakfast had been. Every passion that had burned deep inside her last night had been reignited with the fire burning even hotter. A brand new fantasy invaded her consciousness, one where he was making love to her in a mountain meadow with the warmth of the sun heating their skin and the heat of their passion consuming everything else. It was a brief kiss, but it packed a wallop. Once again, she was left wanting more—a lot more.

But as much as she wanted things to continue, it wasn't possible. Nick had a schedule to keep and it was time to get on with the day's activity.

Everyone saddled up for the return ride, a beautiful trail that wound through a wooded area. As soon as they were out in the open again, everyone had an opportunity to run their horses, ride at a comfortable gallop or continue to walk, depending on their level of expertise and what they felt comfortable with.

Lexi urged her horse into a run even though it had been a long time since she had ridden. She allowed the horse free rein, letting it run as fast as it wanted. The wind whipped through her hair, the breeze hit her face and the sun warmed her skin. The exhilaration filled her with a sense of freedom and carefree fun—feelings she had not indulged in for a long time. And it was all surprisingly comfortable and very real.

When she had left Chicago, enjoyment was definitely not part of her plan nor was a dude ranch her idea of a real vacation. She had been wrong on both counts. Was it the only thing she had been wrong about or was she merely trying to assuage her feelings of guilt? These questions kept repeating in her mind, and the possible answer became more and more disturbing with each passing minute.

The lead wrangler brought the group to a halt and waited for the stragglers to catch up. Then they headed back into the woods and emerged within sight of the corral. A few minutes later, the breakfast ride was over.

Nick took the reins of Lexi's horse and handed them to one of the ranch hands along with his own horse. He walked with her as they casually made their way toward the main lodge building.

"How did you enjoy the ride? I noticed you really had your horse in high gear there for a while."

She bubbled with enthusiasm, the type of sensation she had not felt in a long time. "It was great." She allowed a moment of reflection to temper that excitement. "Of course, I'll probably have some very sore muscles in the morning."

A sly grin turned up the corners of his mouth. "I'll tell

you what.'' He leaned over to whisper in her ear, ''I'll massage that soreness and all those kinks away.'' His lips nibbled at her earlobe. ''I still have that bottle of fine wine and then there's my hot tub.'' He nuzzled the side of her neck before placing a soft kiss behind her ear. ''Did I mention how good a hot tub feels on sore muscles?''

She closed her eyes and a soft moan of pleasure escaped her lips. ''Mmm…that does sound inviting.''

''Good. Then we have a date after dinner tonight?''

His question jolted her back to her purpose for being at the ranch. She took a couple of steps away in order to distance herself from him. ''I'm sure that won't be necessary. I'll work out the soreness at the swimming pool this afternoon.'' She made a hasty decision to take the path that led to the right rather than continue on toward the main lodge building with him. ''I…uh…think I'll go back to my cabin and write some of these postcards that I bought. I'd like to get them in the afternoon mail.''

''Yeah…sure. I'll see you later.'' There was no mistaking the disappointment in his voice or the perplexed expression on his face.

Lexi hurried to her cabin. Things were becoming too confused. She had watched everything he had done and not just that morning, either. She had watched the previous afternoon when he didn't know she was there. She had carefully observed him at dinner that night. There was no way you could call him irresponsible or callous. She could not imagine him knowingly abandoning his son or telling the boy's mother to get out of his life. She felt herself frown as she tried to get a handle on the truth. Her confused feelings all swirled together until they became so entangled that she couldn't separate them.

Marnie had told her one thing. She observed something completely different. And the most devastating aspect of it all was her sense of guilt for her personal involvement with the very man she had come to confront. What was she to believe? Her sister's accusations or her own perceptions of a man who made her tingle with excitement and caused her heart to sing. He had touched an emotional chord deep inside her with such an astonishing swiftness that she was not sure of the precise moment when it happened.

She did not find any pretense, arrogance or mean-spiritedness about him. He seemed genuine from the brim of his Stetson to the toes of his cowboy boots—kind of a ''what you see is what you get'' persona. But which one was the real Nick Clayton—the one Marnie described or the one Lexi observed?

She felt herself being drawn deeper and deeper into a quagmire that was as much emotional as it was physical, a downward spiral she felt powerless to stop—one she was not sure she even wanted to stop. It was no longer a simple case of lust. Somewhere along the line it had turned into more. But how much more? And how long would she be able to keep up this pretense?

Four

Nick watched from his office window as a breathtaking vision named Lexi Parker executed a dive from the board, then swam half the length of the pool underwater, eventually bobbing back to the surface. She ran her fingers through her wet hair to smooth it away from her face, then swam to the side of the pool and climbed out. He continued to watch as the beauty in the red bikini repeated the dive several times before finally claiming one of the lounge chairs and stretching out in the sun.

He watched her for a few seconds longer, then turned away from the window. His mind had been on that morning's breakfast ride ever since they returned. He had tried to finish up some office work, but to no avail.

He liked what he saw and he certainly liked what he touched, but he did not understand her...not at all. One minute, she was warm and soft, cradled in his arms, sharing a passion that almost knocked his socks off. The next, she turned a cool shoulder toward him and backed away as if being with him was the last thing she wanted.

In the past he would have simply moved on rather than spend any more time on what could only be called a losing proposition. But Lexi Parker had grabbed him as no one else ever had. He was willing to work harder in the hope of winning her over. What he was not sure of was his motive, and that bothered him. Oh, sure…she was a beautiful and desirable woman who stirred his passion, and the prospect of making love to her made his heart pound and his blood rush hot and fast through his veins. But was there more to it than just a physical attraction? He didn't have a ready answer for that question and that bothered him, too.

He finished the paperwork left over from the day before, then he wandered toward the pool, making every attempt to appear calm and casual. He paused along the way to speak with the guests and in general be a gracious host, all the while moving steadily in Lexi's direction.

He came to a halt next to her lounge chair, his body casting a shadow across her. He took a steadying breath in hopes of forcing the huskiness out of his voice before he spoke. "You'd better let me put a little sunscreen on you or you'll end up with quite a burn."

If he thought she looked great in cutoffs and a T-shirt, it was nothing compared to the jolt of excitement he felt at that precise moment. The tightness pulled across his chest again and the heat settled low in his body. No woman had ever had this kind of effect on him.

"The mountain air can cause the sun to do funny things to you. You don't realize how much you're getting until it's too late."

She kept her eyes closed, though a slight smile curved her mouth. "It's been such a lazy afternoon. I don't know when I've felt so relaxed. I think I could just stay right here forever." It had been a casual comment spoken light-heartedly, but it lingered in her mind, conjuring up other questions.

What would it be like to live on a ranch? Would she get bored without the amenities offered by the big city? Interesting things to think about, but they were nothing more than idle speculation without any relevance to her life...at least that's what she tried to make herself believe.

Nick reached for the bottle of lotion on the table next to her, took off the cap, then seated himself on the edge of her chair. "You look like you've had enough sun on this side. Why don't you turn over and I'll get your back for you?"

Lexi opened her eyes, using her hand to shade them from the sun. She didn't say anything as she turned onto her stomach. Strong hands gently rubbed the lotion on her skin—intriguing and tantalizing that such a strong man should be able to manifest such a soft touch. And it felt so good. She closed her eyes, and her thoughts drifted to what he'd said about that bottle of fine wine and his private hot tub. A sensual warmth flowed through her body.

Nick and Lexi remained by the pool. They talked quietly, Nick trying to figure out why she seemed to vacillate between warm and cool in her attitude toward him. For Lexi's part, she had abandoned trying to decide what was real and what was not where Nick Clayton was concerned, at least for the time being. He was a truly exciting man, perhaps the most exciting man she had ever encountered. She felt comfortable, content and pleased with the delightful day. It had been so perfect she had almost forgotten about the seriousness of the task that had brought her there.

"Hey, Nick!"

Lexi looked up at the sound of the male voice and saw Danny Clayton approaching, a worried expression on his face.

Danny paused long enough to throw an appreciative look in Lexi's direction, then turned his attention to his brother. "We've got a situation over by the stables that I think you need to handle."

A hint of irritation edged Nick's response. "I'm occupied right now. Can't you take care of it?"

"I really think it needs your authoritative touch." Danny again glanced at Lexi, this time looking apologetic.

Nick turned to Lexi, his words clipped and rushed—almost brusque. "Apparently duty calls. I'll see you later."

Nick and Danny left the pool area and hurried toward the stables. As soon as they were out of earshot of any of the guests, Nick let out his anger and frustration. These feelings had been building inside him for quite a while and Danny had picked the wrong time to rile him.

"Why is it that every little thing gets dumped on me? What is so damned important that you can't take care of it yourself?"

"It's a personnel problem. I thought you ought to be the one to take charge. We caught Tony drinking on the job again. He was in the tack room polishing off the last of his second six-pack of the day."

"And just why does that require *my* immediate attention? Tony knew if he was caught again, he'd be out the door."

Nick and Danny entered the tack room where their foreman, Ken Danzinger, was waiting with an obviously drunk ranch hand. Tony's face contorted into an angry mask. He jumped to his feet when he saw the Clayton brothers approaching, the set of his jaw saying he was ready for a fight.

Nick glared at Tony, then turned his attention to the foreman. "Thanks, Ken. You'd better get the work schedule rearranged to cover Tony's duties."

"Sure thing, Nick." Ken left the tack room, closing the door behind him.

Tony's attitude was defiant, his words thickly slurred. "What the hell's goin' on here? A man can't take a little coffee break without someone jumpin' down his throat?"

Nick met Tony's defiance head-on with a harsh stance of his own. "If you had been drinking coffee, there wouldn't be a problem. Now pack up your stuff and get out. You're through."

Tony lunged toward Nick, taking a swing at him but missing completely as Nick deftly sidestepped the attack while grabbing Tony's arm and twisting it behind his back.

Tony struggled to escape his predicament. "Let go of me, you…"

Nick kept firm control of the situation. "Not until you calm down." Tony continued to struggle and Nick tightened his grip. "I don't want to hurt you, Tony. Now settle down."

Tony finally stopped resisting. When Nick was satisfied that Tony wouldn't start up again, he released his hold on him.

Tony took a couple of steps toward the door while rubbing his arm where Nick had grabbed him. "Look, I'm real sorry about this. It won't happen again." He opened the door and stepped outside as if everything was settled.

Nick and Danny followed him outside. "Not so fast, Tony," Nick called to him. "That doesn't change anything. You're through here. Now pack up your things and vacate the premises."

A look of genuine surprise darted across Tony's face. "What do you mean? I told you it wouldn't happen again."

Nick's patience had been stretched to the limit. He was already upset with Danny for not handling the situation himself. And now Tony seemed to be determined to give him additional grief over a cut-and-dried matter.

Nick fixed him with a hard stare. "The first time you were verbally warned in private so no one else would know about it. At that time you apologized and said it would never happen again. Two months later you were caught drinking during your work hours and you were officially warned, in writing—a form that you countersigned saying you had been put on notice that the next such incident would result in your immediate dismissal. Again you apologized and said it would never happen again. Well, that was a short three weeks ago, wasn't it? I'd say there's nothing left to discuss."

"Oh, yeah?" Tony's voice grew loud, reaching far beyond the immediate area of their confrontation. "Well, you listen to me. I'll get a lawyer and—"

"No! You listen to *me*." Nick's features contorted with the anger that had been seething inside him. "This isn't a matter of you and me having a difference of opinion. As the owners of the Via Verde, we are responsible for the safety of our guests. They come here expecting to have a good time. Some are experienced riders and some are complete novices who've never been out of the city and don't know which end of the horse takes in the oats and which end dispenses them after they've been used.

"It's our job to see that they don't get hurt. I don't have any room for someone who doesn't take that responsibility very seriously. I no longer can depend on you to make sure cinch straps are properly tightened and the guests have reliable supervision.''

He whirled around toward his brother and barked out an order. ''Danny…stay here and *assist* Tony in packing his belongings.'' There was no mistaking Nick's meaning that he didn't want Tony left alone. ''I'll have Mom draw up his final check.'' Nick shot one last hard look at Tony, then walked off toward the office.

Nick's words reached more than Danny's and Tony's ears. Lexi had been on her way back to her cabin when she saw the three men exit the tack room and heard the ongoing argument. She didn't know what started it or specifically why Danny had involved Nick in it, but Nick's anger came through loud and clear. She stopped to listen, guiltily looking around to see if anyone was watching her.

His subject matter caught her attention even more than his obvious anger. He talked about responsibility and its importance. It touched her heart as much as it did her sense of right and wrong. It left her with a warm feeling deep inside and dramatically reinforced what she had come to recognize as her growing emotional involvement. Surely a man that adamant about responsibility in the workplace couldn't be callous and irresponsible in his personal life.

But she had her own responsibilities, too—responsibilities to her nephew, Jimmy; responsibilities to Marnie's memory and the promise she had made to that memory; responsibilities that seemed to be in direct conflict with her own desires.

It was yet another piece of the puzzle that seemed to be evolving into an entirely different picture than she had anticipated. This dilemma attacked the very core of who she was and what she believed in. What she *had* been doing and what she *should* be doing were becoming more and more confused in her mind. Perhaps she needed to redefine her quest.

Her purpose in being at the ranch was not to accuse Nick Clayton or to avenge her sister. It was to do what was best for Jimmy. If that meant making Nick Clayton accept financial responsibility for his son, then that's the way it had to be, regardless of her growing emotional involvement with him. However, if it meant determining that Nick Clayton had no liability in the matter, then she should be able to accept that without feeling as if she had failed Marnie. Another twinge of guilt invaded her consciousness. Unfortunately, that was easier to say than to do.

Lexi continued on to her cabin, showered and dressed for dinner. It had been, without a shadow of a doubt, the most relaxing afternoon she had ever spent. The pool had been refreshing, the sun felt good against her skin, and Nick had been charming and attentive. The more she was around him, the more he impressed her with who and what he was—and the more her sense of guilt plagued her.

She again reflected on his lecture about responsibility. How did that fit with what Marnie had told her? She could not reconcile the two extremes and was leaning more and more toward the conclusion that Marnie had lied about this, just as she had lied about so many other things. Her unexpected yet very real attraction to Nick Clayton made her realize that if she couldn't make any sense of it sometime very soon, she would end up with a problem larger than the one she arrived with.

She hurried to the dining room and was seated at the same table as the night before, except this time Gloria Clayton acted as the hostess. She spotted Nick at another table. He smiled at her and gave her a quick wink before returning his attention to the ranch guests at his table.

Gloria was every bit as charming as her older son. The two women formed an immediate rapport, but Lexi carefully avoided asking any questions about Nick. The last thing she wanted was for either Gloria or Nick to think she was prying into his personal life. The evening passed quickly and soon people were moving next door to the Hoedown Saloon.

Before Lexi could rise from her chair, Nick appeared at her side. "How are those sore muscles?"

An amused chuckle escaped her throat. "I'm okay, but they're letting me know they don't appreciate the workout I gave them this morning."

He held her chair for her, then escorted her toward the door. As soon as they stepped outside, he took her hand as they walked along the path. "I still have that bottle of fine wine. The hot tub is on a timer—" he glanced at his watch "—and it should be turning on just about now. By the time you grab your swimsuit from your cabin and we get to mine, it should be just about ready."

He didn't wait for her to respond and she offered no objection. The moment produced a truth as real as if it had been spoken aloud—she knew they would be making love that night. She had never thrown caution to the wind like this before...she had never made love with a man she had known for such a short time. They walked together to her cabin. Making love with Nick Clayton felt so very right, but she couldn't rid herself of the guilt over Marnie and Jimmy.

She paused a moment before unlocking the door. There was still time to change her mind and put a stop to the direction things were headed. *If* that was what she wanted to do. It was certainly what she *should* do, but not what she wanted. She unlocked the cabin door, stepped inside and flipped on the light.

She turned to Nick, who stood right behind her. The nervous tension in the pit of her stomach had been somewhat under control until the moment she saw the sensual glow flickering in his blue eyes. He looked so desirable and self-assured without being arrogant. She wished she felt half as confident as he looked. She must have surely lost her mind to even be considering this and especially with a man she knew was wrong for her in every way in spite of how very right he seemed.

"I'll get my swimsuit from the towel rack in the bathroom." She heard the anxiety in her voice. She forced a smile, hoping it would calm her nerves. "I hung it there to dry, but it's probably still a little damp from this afternoon's swim." She hurried toward the bathroom before he had a chance to respond.

She could not lie to herself. She could not deny how much she wanted Nick Clayton. Thoughts of Marnie and little Jimmy sent yet another jab of guilt through her. She knew she was digging herself deeper and deeper into a hole. She did not know how to rationalize what she was about to do. But she realized that somehow she would have to find a way.

Her hand trembled slightly as she took her bathing suit from the rack. She grabbed the matching terry-cloth cover-up, then returned to the other room where Nick was waiting for her.

He cocked his head and arched a questioning eyebrow. "Are you ready?"

His voice sounded as confident as he looked. She took a steadying breath to still the butterflies in her stomach. There was time to change her mind. She attempted to sound calm. "Yes, I think so."

She hoped she would not live to regret this decision. She suspected this was standard procedure for Nick—a bottle of wine and a hot tub for two—but it was much more for her. It was a very big step, one cradled in emotion as much as physical desire—perhaps more emotion than she could handle. Perhaps too much emotion.

He flashed a reassuring smile. "Then let's go. The hot tub is bubbling and the wine is chilled. Both should be good medicine for those sore muscles." It almost seemed to her that the comment about her sore muscles had been an afterthought, an attempt to mask the real reason why they were going to his cabin. He again took her hand as they walked along the path.

Nick Clayton may have looked the picture of composure, but it was a far cry from the anxiety running rampant inside him. He felt strangely vulnerable and at a loss. What was there about this woman that had him turned inside out? What did she want? What did she need? Would he be able to please her? These were questions that did not normally accompany his liaisons, but suddenly the doubts surfaced. Why would he have these concerns now?

He unlocked the door to his cabin, then stood aside as Lexi entered. She looked around, surprised by the sight that greeted her. "This is a whole house, isn't it? I thought it would be more like the guest cabins."

He escorted her into the living room, closing the door behind them. "It's my house. Even I get days off from work and need a place I can call home, where I don't have to eat in the guest dining room, watch television in the public lounge—" he paused a moment as a sexy grin tugged at the corners of his mouth "—or use the Jacuzzi out by the pool to get the kinks out of my sore muscles."

He opened the sliding doors to the patio, then turned

on the CD player to a selection of soft mood music. Placing his hand at the small of her back, he directed her toward the hallway, coming to a halt at one of the doors.

"You can change into your swimsuit here if you like, while I change into mine." He turned on the bathroom light for her, then proceeded on down the hallway. She quickly changed into the same red bikini she had worn earlier, then put on the terry-cloth wrap and tied the sash at her waist. She drew in a steadying breath, then returned to the living room.

She immediately spotted Nick in the kitchen opening a bottle of wine. As good as he looked in a denim shirt and tight jeans, he looked a thousand times better in nothing but a swimsuit. She felt a sudden flush of embarrassment heat her cheeks at the blatant nature of her thoughts, but she couldn't ignore his broad shoulders and strong arms, well-defined hard chest, flat stomach and long, muscular legs.

Nick turned when he heard her. "Wine coming up—if you'd like to go out to the patio, I'll be there in just a minute." He took a couple of wineglasses from the cupboard, put ice in a bucket, then added the bottle of white wine.

She managed to produce a weak smile, although she could still feel the heated flush across her cheeks as she stepped through the doorway to the patio. She had fantasized about this from the moment she first saw him, before she even knew who he was, but now that initial surge of heated desire was turning to stomach-churning trepidation.

This wasn't just some fantasy; it was for real. She watched the water bubble in the hot tub and the steam rise into the air. Was it too late to turn and run back to the safety of her own cabin? It wasn't the physical intimacy that scared her; it was the inevitable emotional impact and the ever-present guilt that refused to completely leave her alone. A moment later, she felt his lips on the side of her neck and all her doubts disappeared into the air along with the rising steam. She turned to face him as she untied the sash at her waist, allowing the cover-up to fall open.

Nick set the ice bucket and glasses on the decking that surrounded the edge of the hot tub. He slipped his arms inside the cover-up. His hands slid across the bare skin at her waist, then he pulled her into his embrace. The passion of his kiss left no confusion about where the night was headed. Lexi could no more resist this man than she could resist the need to breathe.

He broke off the kiss but did not release her from his arms. "The hot tub is ready and so is the wine." He brushed his lips against hers again, then indicated the hot bubbling water. "Shall we?" He slipped the terry-cloth cover-up from her shoulders, allowing it to fall to the floor.

Nick paused a moment, cradled Lexi's face in his hands and captured her mouth in a soft kiss. He slipped his tongue between her lips, gently probing and exploring the dark recesses of her mouth. Every second heated his desire closer to the boiling point. He had never been with anyone quite like her. Her taste produced a feeling of euphoria unlike any he had ever experienced before. It was almost akin to an addictive drug—each taste demanded more.

She returned his movements, twining her tongue with his, reveling in the texture of his mouth pressed against hers. Nothing mattered at that moment other than Nick Clayton and the excitement that welled inside her each time they came into physical contact no matter how fleeting the touch. Once again, feelings of guilt created thoughts of her sister and little Jimmy, but she shoved them away as quickly as they appeared.

A shiver of sweet anticipation darted across the surface of her skin. He pressed his lips against the side of her throat, nibbled at the juncture of her neck and shoulder, then brushed the tip of his tongue along the ridge of her shoulder blade. She trailed her hands across his hard chest, allowing her fingertips to linger on his strong heartbeat.

He took her hand and helped her into the hot tub, then joined her in the water swirling around their bodies. The sensation increased the air of excitement that already surrounded them. Nick poured two glasses of wine and handed one to her.

She accepted the glass. "Thank you." She took a sip then surveyed the patio area. The silence became awkward for her and she felt pressured to say something…anything. "This water sure feels good. You're right about a hot tub being very therapeutic for sore muscles. If you get thrown from those bucking horses very often, I would imagine that you spend a lot of time here."

"I average four or five times a week. If it's been a particularly rough day, this is a good place to unwind."

She heard the touch of seriousness settle over what had been a smooth and seductive tone of voice. She wasn't quite sure exactly how to respond to it. "I suppose, like any business, this one has its good days and its bad days."

"Yes. There were some bad moments this afternoon, but they're behind me now." His sexy smile returned. "This has turned out to be one of the good ones." He raised his glass in a toast. Even in the dim light, she could see the desire that sparkled in his eyes. His soft words caressed her senses. "To a very lovely lady who has graciously consented to spend the evening with me."

His words thrilled Lexi to the very core of her being. Her heart pounded just a little faster and her pulse quickened. The full implication of his words sent a rush of desire through her body. She was thankful for the subdued lighting, grateful that he was not able to see the flush of embarrassment she felt spreading across her cheeks as she listened to his words.

They sipped their wine. The soft music filtering through from the living room enhanced the sounds of bubbling water. The magical moment was alive with the heady ambiance which drew them closer and closer. By the time they had finished their wine, they were involved in a deliciously earthy kiss and a tangle of arms and legs.

Nick deftly untied the straps at the back of her neck, allowing them to fall from her shoulders. A sudden rush of warm water invaded the bikini top and caressed her bare skin. Then his hand cupped the curve of her exposed breast, causing a ripple of pleasure to course through her and a soft moan of delight to escape her throat.

His voice thickened with passion. "I'll pour us another glass of wine. But first—" he reached behind her and unfastened the last bit of fabric holding her bikini top together "—let's get rid of this." He placed it on the decking next to the ice bucket.

She had never experienced such a tantalizing seduction in her entire life. Regardless of her compelling reasons for being at the Via Verde Dude Ranch in the first place, she could not deny a growing and very powerful emotional entanglement with Nick Clayton. It was something quite different from her overwhelming need for him to make love to her. Would she ever be able to rationalize this decision in the clear and revealing light of dawn?

Enveloped in a cloud of steam they were unable to keep their hands off each other. The tantalizing excitement and sexual tension built to a feverish pitch as their bodies responded to each intimate touch and soft caress.

His excitement grew and expanded, his arousal hardened, as he watched the bubbling water trickle across her breasts. Her taut nipples peeked out, only to be quickly covered again by the water. He pulled her on top of him and wrapped her body in his embrace. He claimed her mouth with a heated passion that made the water seem cool by comparison. Moments later, his swimsuit and the rest of hers joined the bikini top in a wet heap on the decking.

He nuzzled the side of her neck, then whispered in her ear, his voice husky with the urgency of his desire. ''I think we've been in the water long enough.''

An equal amount of passion filled her words. ''I think so, too.''

She shivered as the cool air hit her wet skin when she stood up. He grabbed her cover-up and wrapped it around her. He scooped her up in his arms, a trail of water marking the path he took as he carried her down the hallway and gently deposited her in the middle of his bed.

The image exactly duplicated what he had visualized in his mind's eye when he'd first seen her. Lexi was stretched out on his bed with her long blond hair spread out across his pillow. Her hazel eyes sparkled with excitement and her slightly parted kiss-swollen lips invited him to taste more.

Five

Lexi's insides quivered with excitement as Nick's gaze traveled over her body. His blue eyes sparkling with desire caused her to tingle with sweet anticipation. She felt deliciously wanton. She did not know what the future held and at that moment did not want to dwell on it, but if this was to be their only night of passion, she wanted it to be enough to remain in her memory forever. She didn't want to think about the deeper feelings and emotions that were crystallizing inside her—nor did she want to think about the problems they represented.

She had Jimmy's welfare to take care of and the vow she had made at Marnie's funeral. She shook away the intrusive thoughts. She had made her decision. She would just have to figure out how to live with the consequences of that decision—whatever they might be. But for tonight, Nick Clayton embodied everything she wanted.

He stretched out on the bed next to her. As he ran his

fingertips across the swell of her breasts, he whispered in her ear, "I'm sure you've heard this many times before, but it's worth repeating. You're a very beautiful woman and incredibly desirable." He dipped his head and drew her hardened nipple into his mouth, holding it there for a second as his tongue explored the puckered bud.

She wrapped her arms around him, caressing his tautly muscled back and broad shoulders. Was any of this real? She certainly didn't make a habit of jumping into bed with men she had only known for a couple of days. So what was she doing in Nick Clayton's bed? Nothing about any of this made sense to her, except that no one made her blood race the way he did. She was afraid to think about what he was doing to her emotions but couldn't keep her thoughts from straying to the future and a lifetime commitment...and whether that future could possibly include Nick Clayton.

Any further concerns and doubts disappeared in an incendiary rush of excitement as he stroked her inner thigh, then slowly drew his fingertips through the downy softness covering her femininity. A gasp of pleasure caught in her throat when he captured her mouth with a kiss so intense that it made his previous kisses pale in comparison. His mouth demanded, his tongue insisted, and she responded with a fervor every bit the equal to his.

His rigid manhood pressed against her leg, letting her know that he was as ready as she was. She reached for his fully aroused sex. Just as her hand made contact with his hardness, her body convulsed in ecstasy when he slipped his finger between the moist folds of her womanhood. She arched her hips and shoved against his hand, wanting more of the delicious sensations and more of Nick Clayton.

His fingers left a heated wake wherever they came in

contact with her skin as he expertly explored every nuance of her body. He trailed kisses down the side of her neck and across the swell of her breast, culminating in the most intimate touch of all as his mouth brushed against her femininity. The depth of his passion elevated her to new heights of ecstasy. It was incredibly real, somehow transcending even her most torrid fantasies.

As Lexi trembled with pleasure, he reached for the drawer in the nightstand, removed a packet and quickly made use of the contents. He hesitated a moment, caught off guard by a sudden wave of panic that materialized from out of nowhere and crashed through his consciousness with a vengeance. He quickly captured her mouth with a kiss hot enough to burn away the unwelcome doubts and fears. He thrust his hips forward as she lifted hers to meet him.

The precise moment of their physical joining sent a heated jolt through his body unlike anything he had ever experienced before. The sensation was almost overwhelming, but there was something more…something so subtle that he couldn't define it, yet something so real that it frightened him.

He set a smooth rhythm that quickly escalated as they each succumbed to the strength of the physical responses rapidly building inside them, layer upon layer. Their frenzied actions reached a peak as a series of convulsions claimed Lexi, then Nick's body stiffened as he tightened his arms around her.

The hard spasms ripped through him. He gave one final thrust deep inside her, then held her tightly in his arms until he was finally at rest. He kissed her forehead, then brushed aside a loose tendril of hair from where it clung to her damp cheek. He again wrapped her in his arms and held her body close to his. It felt so very right, more than it ever had before with any other woman.

He continued to hold her, not knowing what to say and afraid to say anything. His desire for Lexi had been all-consuming. He knew it was more than just raging hormones, but he had not been prepared for just how much more. He had never felt that much at one with another human being in his life. It was so far removed from simple sex that he didn't even know how to categorize it. In fact, he wasn't all that sure he wanted to categorize it. This time he wanted more than just a quick roll in the hay or a hot, fast affair that would only last a couple of weeks, but the thought of how much more that might be truly frightened him. He was not ready to face that yet.

He watched her for a moment. A thin sheen of perspiration still covered her face and shoulders. The flush of the sensual afterglow belonging to the quiet moments following lovemaking spread across her cheeks. Her breasts rose and fell with her breathing. He liked the idea of waking up in the morning and finding her at his side, yet at the same time the notion caused another disturbing surge of panic. He closed his eyes and tried to quell the disquieting thoughts and feelings.

Lexi remained very still with her eyes closed. Perhaps Nick would think she was asleep, giving her time to try to reason things through. She had just made love with the last man on earth she should be intimately involved with...and the most exciting man she had ever known. Is that how it had been with Marnie? Had Nick worked his magic charms on her in much the same manner? Was she about to follow in her sister's disastrous footsteps where the persuasive and sexy Nick Clayton was concerned?

She had thought that following the experience of her own broken engagement from a man who turned out to be a two-timing louse would have been enough to keep her from ever trusting anyone with her emotions ever again. That belief had been reinforced by the example of her sister's two failed marriages. But now she found herself in a true quandary and didn't know what to think. She did know that one word kept circulating through her mind, and as much as she didn't want it to be there, that one word was *love*.

How could everything have happened so quickly? Was Nick feeling anything close to the same level of emotional involvement that had hit her, or for him had this only been about sex? And what did this do to her sworn objective? Had she totally compromised any attempt to get at the truth about Nick and Marnie? Would she be able to overcome her feelings of guilt or would they be her undoing? She had many questions but no answers. The one thing she did know for sure was that she was in way over her head and didn't know how to get out.

She remained enveloped by his arms, afraid to open her eyes and face reality—afraid to break the enchanted moment that held her in its spell. How could things be so perfect yet so terrible at the same time?

Lexi slowly became cognizant of being awake. She remained still with her eyes closed as she replayed each delicious moment of the previous night in her mind. Her body still tingled from the afterglow of the second time they had made love about three o'clock that morning. She had turned over on her side and a moment later Nick's hand had slid across her midriff, then cupped her breast. He hadn't needed to ask if she was awake since she had immediately responded by running her foot along his leg. Their earlier lovemaking had been magical, but the next time had been earth-shattering. The euphoria still clung to her senses as she lazily slid her hand across the sheet and reached out toward him.

Her eyes popped open the moment she realized she was in bed alone. She looked around the bedroom, but Nick was nowhere in sight. Where had he gone? Had he simply walked off without giving her a second thought, just assuming she would return to her own cabin when she woke up? Was Nick Clayton's *true* character finally showing through? Had he completely taken her in with his irresistible charm and smooth manner? Was he really the person Marnie had described to her rather than the one she thought she had come to know—or the one she just might be falling in love with?

The aroma of freshly brewed coffee wafted to her senses and a moment later Nick appeared at the door wearing only a pair of jogging shorts and carrying a tray. She could not stop the soft smile that came to her lips. She knew in an instant that her feelings for him had infinitely increased. In the clear light of dawn, there was no doubt in her mind that she was well on her way to being hopelessly in love with Nick Clayton, regardless of the concerns that circulated through her mind. She allowed herself to indulge the warm feeling of contentment a moment longer, one that enveloped her much like a warm cocoon.

He placed the tray on the nightstand, then seated himself next to her on the bed. His presence was as welcome as the early-morning sun that filtered in through the bedroom drapes. He leaned forward and brushed a gentle kiss across her lips. "Good morning." He reached out and lightly stroked her cheek, tucking a stray lock of hair behind her ear. "Did you sleep well?"

She stretched her legs out beneath the sheet and arched her back. She smiled lazily. Her words came out thickly, giving evidence to the fact that she had just woken up. "Yes, I did. And you?"

"Never better."

Her smile faded as the reality of the morning after began to seep into her consciousness. What had been blissful contentment only a moment ago had suddenly become serious. Her words were hesitant. She was not sure how to express what was on her mind.

"About last night…" She rose to a sitting position and drew her knees up in front of her, being careful to keep herself covered with the sheet. "I don't want you to think I'm accustomed to hopping into bed…" She nervously ran her fingers through her hair in an attempt to smooth it away from her face. "That I routinely sleep with men I've only known for a couple of—"

He stilled her words with his fingertips as he searched the depth of her eyes. "I never for a moment thought that."

He sounded so sincere, his expression honest and forthright. She hoped he was telling her the truth. Everything she had observed about Nick Clayton said he was a man who did not trade in pretense or phoniness. Was it her own confused feelings of guilt that were making her question things?

Before she could delve any further into her unsettling thoughts, Nick pulled her into his embrace and held her close. His words whispered across her senses. "Thank you for last night. You are truly a very special lady." He cradled her head against his shoulder, savoring the closeness of the moment before saying anything else. "This is my day off. Would you spend it with me? I'd love to show you the ranch—places the guests never get to see. There's a waterfall not too far from here. We can take a picnic lunch and…"

He couldn't finish. Instead, he sought out her lips and placed an emotion-filled kiss on them. He knew something very profound had happened when he made love to Lexi, but he didn't know exactly what it was. In fact, he was not sure he even wanted to know. He didn't have room in his life for complications.

"A picnic by a waterfall sounds like a marvelous idea." Any suggestion he made would have sounded like a marvelous idea to Lexi as long as they were together. She had to learn more about him. She was amazed at how open about himself and his life he had already been. It didn't seem to matter what she asked him; he willingly told her whatever she wanted to know. He seemed to be a man with a clear conscience and nothing to hide—certainly not the man Marnie had described to her.

Her ever-increasing guilt became a double-edged sword. Not only had she betrayed her vow to her sister, but she had not been honest with Nick, either. She managed to dismiss the concern as not relevant at the moment. In fact, perhaps it wasn't relevant at all. There simply couldn't be any way that this man would knowingly desert a woman carrying his child—no way at all. And in light of this, to confront him with her sister's story would be humiliating for her and embarrassing to him. It would serve no purpose and was better off left alone. She would put it out of her mind and get on with her life.

A sudden doubt assailed her. Would it really be that easy?

Nick handed her a cup of coffee, bringing her attention back to the here and now, then poured one for himself. She sipped her coffee while listening to the plans he'd made for them. His animated expression matched a voice filled with enthusiasm as he shared with her his eagerness for the day's adventure. It all seemed so natural and right, the two of them sitting on the bed together planning what they would do that day.

He took her empty coffee cup and set it on the tray, then grasped her hand and playfully tugged until she was out of bed and on her feet. ''We have a busy day ahead and need to get moving. Would you like to have breakfast here or in the dining hall?''

''Either way, I need to go to my cabin. All I have here is this—'' she slipped on her cover-up, using it as a robe ''—and a swimsuit that's still out by the hot tub.''

He slid his hands inside the wrap, skimming his fingers across the perfect roundness of her bare bottom before pulling her hips tightly against his. His mouth came down hard on hers, rekindling all the passion of the previous night. It didn't take long before they were both back in bed, once again sharing the heated desires that neither of them could ignore—the desires she feared would be her downfall.

Nick tethered the horses, allowing them enough line to graze in the meadow, while Lexi spread the picnic blanket on the grass. She wasn't sure when or how he'd done it, but while she was back in her cabin showering and changing clothes, he had somehow managed to acquire a picnic basket packed with delicious-looking goodies. She started to set out the food, then paused as she turned to watch him.

His every movement exuded a self-assuredness she wished she possessed, the type that left everyone around him feeling confident that things were in very capable hands. She thought it surely must be comforting to see things so clearly and to always know the appropriate thing to do.

Guilt had been growing inside her all morning. How

could she be falling in love with Nick Clayton when she had not yet gotten to the truth about him and Marnie? She feared all the loose ends—the divided loyalties—would come back to haunt her and she didn't know what to do about it. She closed her eyes for a moment, offering up a silent prayer that she wouldn't be forced to make a choice between the man she was falling in love with—and the future that could represent—and the sister she had always loved.

"What's the matter?" He pulled her into his embrace. "You looked like you were in pain. Is something wrong?" He placed a soft kiss on her forehead.

"No…nothing. I was just thinking about a problem at home, something I've been putting off but will have to tackle…eventually…probably." Her voice trailed off. She didn't know how to finish her thought.

He presented a very businesslike and matter-of-fact attitude. "Sorry, but we don't allow our guests to worry about problems at home while they're vacationing at the Via Verde. It's a house rule—no exceptions. The only thing we allow our guests to concentrate on is enjoying their stay with us." He took her hand in his and with the other hand scooped up the picnic basket.

Vacation…if only things were that simple and her presence at the ranch so easily explained. The inner doubts that plagued her thoughts, her growing fear of the shifting emotional tide pulling her in a different direction than she had planned to go—it all weighed heavily on her. She would raise Jimmy and love him and provide him with a secure home; there was no question about that. What she didn't know was how to find that thin dividing line between her love for Nick Clayton and her loyalty to her sister's memory.

His upbeat voice overruled her conflicting feelings, at

least for the moment. "Come on, let's eat. I'm hungry enough to chew the bark off a tree—" he paused long enough for his intense blue eyes to delve into her inner- most existence "—or devour you, body and soul."

They were surrounded by a blanket of emotional elec- tricity, the heated moment drawing them closer together. She closed her eyes and allowed her head to rest against his shoulder. What had she gotten herself into?

She nervously cleared her throat, then attempted to pro- ject the same type of upbeat manner he had displayed. "I took a peek into the picnic basket. Everything looks de- licious."

He gave her a quick wink and a smile as he placed the basket on the blanket. "Our chef tells me it's a feast fit for a queen." He waved his arm toward the blanket in a broad, sweeping gesture. "So...would her majesty care to be seated?"

She returned his warm smile. "Thank you." She sat cross-legged and watched as he unpacked their lunch— fried chicken, a delicious looking salad, cheeses, fresh fruit and some cookies.

Lexi didn't know whether Nick was going out of his way to be charming and agreeable or if it was his true nature, but he managed to ease all her concerns and anx- ieties. After they finished eating, Lexi started clearing away their picnic debris and packing everything in the basket in preparation for the ride back to the stables.

Nick sat under a large tree, his back resting against the trunk and his legs stretched out in front of him. He watched as Lexi put the last remnants of their picnic into the basket and closed the lid. When she turned toward him, he held out his hand to her. "Are you in a hurry to get back?"

She accepted his hand, lacing their fingers together. A

soft smile turned the corners of her mouth. "No, not especially. Why?"

"I thought we could sit under this nice old tree, listen to the birds and the sounds of the waterfall, then decide what we're going to do tonight. There's line dancing scheduled for the Hoedown Saloon with instructions for those who've never done it before. Or—" he tugged on her hand and pulled her down next to him "—we could see where the evening takes us."

Lexi nestled her body between his outstretched legs. He wrapped his arms around her as she rested her back against his chest. She felt safe and secure, as if nothing in the world could ever hurt her. They remained like that for almost an hour, silently enjoying the closeness without needing to fill the quiet time with conversation. It was late that afternoon before they mounted their horses and returned to the stables.

They dropped off the picnic basket at the ranch kitchen, then started to leave. Before they could get out the door, Danny caught up with them.

"Hey, Nick. Wait up. You're just the man I wanted to see."

Nick turned to his brother, immediate skepticism coloring his greeting. "Danny." He put his arm around Lexi's shoulders in an attempt to convey the message that he already had plans. "Is there a problem of some sort?"

"Well..." Danny glanced in Lexi's direction, extending an apologetic look and embarrassed smile before returning his attention to his brother. "Do you want to teach line dancing or be the bartender for the evening?"

"Why?" Nick drew his arm back from Lexi and instantly became all business. "What's the problem?"

"We have several people out sick. Must be some sort of flu bug going around. A couple of the day-shift people have agreed to work a double shift and Mom is handling the front desk. I was about to put up a notice canceling line-dancing lessons, then take over the bar when I saw you. So, which job do you want?''

Nick's brow furrowed. ''Mom is working tonight? I don't like that. She shouldn't be working so many hours. She's not up to it. I want you to go ahead and cancel the line dancing. One of us can work the front desk and the other can tend bar.''

''You'll do no such thing.'' Gloria brought her chair to a halt next to Nick. ''The guests are looking forward to the line dancing and we can't disappoint them. There's no reason why I can't work the front desk this evening.''

Nick projected a degree of control over the situation. ''No way, Mom. It's too much. You need your rest.''

Gloria's spirited nature made itself known, showing a strong-willed woman who may have lost the use of her legs but certainly was not ready to be put out to pasture. ''Nicky…unless you've managed to graduate from medical school while I wasn't looking, I'm going to insist— again—that you stop treating me like an invalid.''

Nick mustered an engaging smile, one that apparently worked well in persuading others to his way of seeing things. ''Now, Mom. You know what Dr. Blanchard said about your needing your rest.''

''That was eight years ago, right after I got out of the hospital. He's long since rescinded that edict. Now, I don't want to hear any more about canceling the line-dancing instructions.'' Gloria started toward the lobby, then turned back to her two sons, who stood staring after her. ''Well, don't just stand there. Let's get to work.''

Lexi watched as Gloria proceeded through the dining hall toward the front lobby, leaving Nick and Danny to take care of their end of things. The two brothers engaged in quiet but obviously serious conversation.

Her few brief conversations with Gloria had been interesting. She was obviously an intelligent and warm woman. But after watching this exchange between the three Claytons, she could definitely see where Nick got his clear-cut sense of responsibility and authoritative manner when it came to running the business. Surely a man raised by this woman would never consider abandoning the woman carrying his child or denying any responsibility for that baby.

Nick turned to Lexi. "I'm sorry. It seems that my day off has just been canceled. I've been elected bartender for the evening. It was the lesser of two evils. Danny will do a much better job of line-dance instruction than I will. He enjoys getting up in front of everyone, showing off and occasionally making a fool of himself while being the center of attention." He put his arm around her shoulders and began walking through the dining hall.

"It looks like I'll be working until at least midnight." He stopped walking when he came to the door connecting the dining hall with the saloon. He ran his fingertips across her cheek, then traced her upper lip. His voice grew soft, his words for her ears only. "This certainly isn't how I planned to spend the night, but duty calls." His tone dropped to an even more intimate level. "Could I persuade you to stop by for a glass of wine and maybe keep me company for a little while tonight?"

"You're a very persuasive man." A little shiver of excitement swept through her body. Yes, very persuasive indeed. She smiled. "I'd like that."

His face beamed with pleasure. "Good. I'll see you later."

As soon as he disappeared through the saloon door, she

wandered in the other direction toward the front lobby. She thought about what had just happened. It was yet another example of his integrity and dedication to duty.

Again she wondered about what Marnie had told her. How much of it was true and how much fabrication? Or— the thought that hurt most of all—was any of Marnie's story true? The doubts that had once been directed against Nick were now swinging around toward her own sister. As each passing hour with Nick produced deeper feelings, it also drove a large wedge between those feelings and the original purpose for her trip to the ranch.

Her fear that this conflict would only bring disaster began to loom large in her consciousness.

Six

Lexi wandered into the front lobby feeling at a bit of a loss about what to do that evening. What had promised to be another passionate night with Nick had suddenly turned into one she'd be spending alone. She had packed a couple of books with her clothes, assuming there'd be nights when she'd be staying in her cabin. She decided to read for a while, then go to the saloon and have that glass of wine with Nick as he had asked.

"Lexi!" Gloria called to her as Lexi started across the lobby. "Do you have a minute?"

Lexi turned at the sound of her name. She smiled upon seeing Gloria. "Of course." She hurried over to the front desk.

Gloria's warmth and charm seemed to come naturally to her, not something she produced to suit the situation. "I'm so sorry to spoil whatever plans you and Nick had for the evening. Six employees called in sick and it really put us in a bind. Two or three can be easily handled, but six is quite another matter.''

Lexi immediately perked up to attention. ''Is there something I can do to help? I was just going back to my cabin to read for a while. I'll be happy to lend a hand.''

''Absolutely not. It's not our policy to put our guests to work.''

Lexi glanced around the lobby, then returned her attention to Gloria. It seemed like a perfect opportunity for them to have a nice chat without anyone else being around. ''This is a lovely vacation spot. Nick told me this used to be a family cattle ranch at one time, then you decided to turn it into a dude ranch.''

''I'm afraid Nick is being a little modest, as usual. This entire thing was his idea and it's successful today primarily because of his hard work and leadership.'' She became reflective for a moment, staring down at her wheelchair as she ran her fingertip along the chair arm. ''After Ed died, it was Nick who held everything together. We wouldn't have made it without his strength and determination.''

''Yes, he seems to be a hard worker—'' she carefully ventured her next comment, not sure exactly where she was going with it, ''—and a very responsible person.''

Gloria laughed. ''Yes, 'responsible' certainly describes Nick. I have one son with an overdeveloped sense of responsibility and another who views life as a playground.

''Nick and Ken Danzinger, our foreman, did a lot of the building renovations themselves while Danny finished his senior year of college. It took almost six months of hard work to get things ready for the change over to a dude ranch. And when we first opened, Nick worked sixteen hours a day, seven days a week. He takes a few days off now and then, but he hasn't had a proper vacation since we opened the doors for business over seven years ago.''

Gloria shot Lexi a knowing look. "I was glad to see him take a day off today. I'm only sorry business needs intruded into that time and spoiled the rest of your plans.''

Lexi felt the slight flush of embarrassment rise on her cheeks. "No problem. When you own your own business, I'm sure that's the type of thing you need to contend with.''

"I think it's going to be a quiet evening for me. Everyone who was scheduled to arrive today has already checked in, so barring any unforeseen emergencies, I should be able to catch up on some of my paperwork.''

"Well, I'd better let you get back to work. See you later.'' Lexi started to leave.

"No need to rush off, unless you have something specific to do.'' Gloria smiled. "I'm always looking for an excuse to put off the boring little paperwork details.'' She wheeled out from behind the desk and headed toward one of the conversational seating arrangements in the lobby.

Lexi settled into a comfortable chair while Gloria turned to face her. Apparently, Gloria wanted some company and Lexi was eager to comply. It would be a perfect opportunity to get some information about Nick. She had already elicited a very valuable piece of information from Gloria about Nick's sense of responsibility and she was anxious to learn more.

"Now, tell me, Lexi…what is it you do for a living?''

"I'm a schoolteacher. I teach eighth-grade English and occasionally fill in with social studies.''

Gloria's expression brightened. "Really? I planned to be a schoolteacher at one time. I graduated from college and was about to go for my teaching certificate when I met Ed.'' A wistful expression crossed her face, a softness that told of fond memories and loving times. "Edward Clayton simply swept me off my feet. There's no way to describe it other than love at first sight. I took one look at him and I was a goner. To everyone's surprise, we were married just three weeks later. We had twenty-five marvelous years together before he died."

Lexi found that to be an interesting coincidence. What Gloria described was almost the identical thing that happened to her when she first saw Nick. Were her feelings of guilt and her concerns about betraying her sister's memory nothing more than a futile effort in the face of such extraordinary happenings? Was this something that happened with all the Clayton men— that women instantly fell in love with them? It was a sobering thought. Was that what happened with Marnie, too?

Gloria's gaze darted around the lobby as if searching for the right words to put to her thoughts. "If it hadn't been for Nick taking charge and he and Danny throwing me into the work involved in creating the dude ranch, I'd probably still be sitting by my window watching the world go by with no purpose or direction to my life."

The two women talked for more than an hour. The brief conversations Lexi had earlier enjoyed with Gloria had been pleasant, but this time there had been a true depth solidifying a new and very real friendship.

A series of phone calls and business matters sent Gloria back to work. Lexi excused herself and returned to her cabin intending to read for a while, then go to the saloon to have that glass of wine with Nick.

She kicked off her shoes, plumped the pillows on the bed, grabbed her book and settled in to read. Her eyes grew heavy. A few minutes later, her book rested against her chest and she was asleep.

* * *

Nick periodically shot anxious glances across the room during the course of the evening. Each time he expected to see Lexi enter the saloon through the swinging wooden doors. And each time he had to swallow his disappointment and return his attention to mixing drinks. He had truly believed that she would join him for that glass of wine and go back to his cabin with him when the saloon closed.

And now it was time. He mechanically handled the closing routines, took the cash drawer from the register and went to the business office. A few minutes later, he left the main building and headed toward his cabin.

At the last moment, almost as an afterthought, he veered off the main path and took the one toward Lexi's cabin. He paused outside her door, noting that her light was on. He knocked softly. When he received no answer, he continued on to his cabin.

He stood in his living room staring out at the hot tub. He vividly recalled each and every detail of their evening that had culminated in a night of making love. He wandered down the hall to his bedroom. He sat on the edge of the bed and ran his hand across the sheets. It had been a night that would never leave his mind, one that had a shockingly profound impact on him. He had made love to more than his share of women, even been infatuated with a couple of them, but this felt different.

He undressed and climbed into bed. Even though he was tired, sleep eluded him. He stared up through the darkness at the ceiling, his mind fully consumed with thoughts of Lexi. He forced his eyes closed. He needed to be at the stables at five-thirty in the morning to fill in for the recently departed Tony. He glanced at the glowing red numerals on the clock. That was only five hours away. He forced his eyes shut again.

He tossed and turned, waking up several times during the night. Each time he reached across the bed thinking he would find Lexi. And each time he found he was alone.

Five o'clock finally arrived. He took a quick shower, dressed, then hurried to the stables to begin his workday. And all the while, his thoughts revolved around Lexi—thoughts about a relationship, thoughts about his true feelings for her...even thoughts of what the future might hold.

He wasn't sure exactly what was happening between them and it bothered him. There had never been a reason for him to give any thought to a serious relationship. Things had been great for the past few years. He lived in one of nature's most spectacular settings doing work he enjoyed. Thanks to the ranch's success, he could afford to indulge his interests and desires. He dated many women and found the variety stimulating. His brow creased in confusion. He didn't understand why thoughts of a serious nature surfaced every time Lexi Parker came to mind, but he needed to rid himself of them.

He knew too many people who'd had their dreams and hopes dashed by bad marriages and an excess of family responsibilities they weren't ready to handle. Things were great just the way they were. He certainly didn't need to make any changes to his life, regardless of how confused he became every time he thought about Lexi.

At least that's what he tried to tell himself. But try as he might, he knew it was all a lie. No one had ever hit him emotionally the way she had. Just the sound of her voice sent a wave of excitement through him. He found her to be intelligent, capable, independent, warm, giving...she was everything any man could want. So why were caution flags waving all around him?

Even though Lexi had neither said nor done anything specific, he couldn't shake the notion that she had a separate agenda of her own for being at the ranch. The feeling had surfaced when they first met and hadn't gone away in spite of their mutual passions that pulled them together tighter than glue.

He toyed with the idea that it might be his imagination or possibly even an excuse to allow him to back off from what was happening. Maybe Lexi's failure to show up at the saloon the previous night had been a sign that she, too, was unsure of things. True, her initial antagonism had vanished, but surely the underlying cause must still be there.

Nick busied himself in the stables, mechanically moving through the morning routine to prepare for the day's activities, but his mind was elsewhere. Before he and Lexi had made love, he believed the only relationship they would have was one based on an intense physical attraction that would last until it was time for her to return home. Now he didn't know what to think…or more accurately, what to do. Somewhere along the line, things had gotten out of hand. It was no longer merely fun and games. The prospect of what might really be happening left him feeling very unsettled.

He forced the disturbing thoughts from his mind and turned his full attention to his work.

Lexi nervously paced up and down her cabin. She could not go on like this, pretending everything was exactly as it should be. What had been the marvelously euphoric feeling of falling in love had edged closer and closer to misery with each passing hour. Try as she might, she could no longer juggle her feelings…balancing her growing love for Nick Clayton with her guilt over betraying her sister's memory.

In her heart, she knew Nick could never have deserted

Marnie and her son, but that didn't resolve the dilemma. She still had another possibility to tackle—that Marnie had never told him she was pregnant. She had to put her personal feelings aside and get to the bottom if things. She needed to know if Nick had taken Marnie to Hawaii as she claimed.

Lexi agonized over how to deal with the situation. One truth was inescapable. No matter what happened, Jimmy was involved. He had to be figured into the equation. If she had any future with Nick, it could only be because he accepted Jimmy as part of that future. Another realization couldn't be ignored—Nick had never mentioned the future. It was a topic they had not discussed. She shook her head. That made no difference to what she needed to do.

Resolute now, she headed for the lobby to find a pay phone. A few minutes later, she had reached her mother.

"I realize it's very short notice, mother. It's just that things here aren't what I thought they would be. I mean…well, nothing is as I had pictured it." She listened to the inevitable "I told you so" as she tried to muster as much calm and control as she could. "Do you suppose we could save that discussion for some other time? Right now there are more important things to consider. As much as I hate to say this, I'm not sure anymore how much truth there is to Marnie's story." She paused as a knot of sadness lodged in her throat. "Assuming there's any truth to it at all."

She heard her mother talking but could not concentrate on the words. She had been so sure when she boarded the plane in Chicago. She knew what needed to be done and had the determination to do it. But now she was not sure of anything.

It took a little bit of effort, but she managed to erase the irritation from her voice. "That's not important right now, Mother. What we need to do is bring this predicament to a close as quickly as possible…one way or the other. I'd like you to bring Jimmy here. If Nick Clayton *is* Jimmy's father, then he should meet his son. And if not…well…it will be a nice experience for Jimmy to be in the mountains and around the horses.'' It wasn't what she had planned to say, but it would have to do. ''Do you think you could be here tomorrow?'' She listened for a moment, not happy with what she heard. ''Okay, then…day after tomorrow.''

She finished her phone call, then returned to her cabin. Confusion and indecision churned in the pit of her stomach, at war with what she felt in her heart for Nick Clayton. Was it destined to be an unrequited love?

She closed her eyes for a moment and tried to get her priorities in order. Jimmy's upbringing and education came before everything else. If Nick was his father, then Nick must be held accountable. Once again the horrible conflict that was tearing her apart grabbed hold of her senses. If it did turn out, despite her belief, that Nick *was* Jimmy's father… She paused as a sob caught in her throat. She couldn't bear the thought of his being such a callous person as to deny his own son's existence. The Nick Clayton she had come to know and love simply could never do that.

She tried to pull herself together. She could not hide in her cabin for two days. She could not hide from Nick, hoping her feelings would somehow change or that she would discover what she thought was love was really nothing more than a temporary infatuation. She put on her swimsuit and headed for the pool. Perhaps the warm sun would carry away the chill that had settled over her.

She hurried along the path while keeping an eye out for Nick, part of her wanting desperately to be in his arms again and part of her wanting to avoid him at least until she'd figured out what to do. She passed the stables and continued on toward the pool.

Lexi had almost reached the pool when Nick spotted her. For hours, ever since daylight, he had kept a close watch for her. He wanted to talk to her…he *needed* to talk to her. He had to satisfy himself that her failure to show up at the saloon the previous night did not signal a rejection. While he was not clear in his mind on where things were going with Lexi, he knew positively that he did not want them to stop.

Nick turned toward Ken Danzinger while keeping track of Lexi from the corner of his eye. "Are you okay here, Ken? I have some other business to handle."

Ken looked around. "Yeah, I'm fine. Thanks for the helping hand. I've got the schedule reworked and we have a new hand starting the first of the week." A wide grin spread across his weathered face. "So I'm afraid your services are no longer required. I'll be sure to give you a good reference, though, if you decide to look for work elsewhere."

Nick fell in with his kidding. "Oh, yeah? Well, I'll have you know I've been fired from better jobs than this." He glanced in the direction of the pool and noticed that Lexi had settled into a lounge chair. "I'll see you later, Ken. Give me a shout if you need anything."

Nick hurried toward the pool area, never taking his eyes off the beautiful vision in the red bikini. He grabbed a chair and pulled it over next to her.

He tried to keep the uneasiness out of his voice even though he couldn't stop the churning in his stomach. He smiled. "Hi. I missed you last night. I was hoping you'd come over to the saloon for a drink."

Lexi flushed with embarrassment. "I went back to my

cabin to read for a while and planned to head over to the saloon a little later. Unfortunately—'' she lowered her gaze for a moment, then regained eye contact with him ''—I must have been more tired than I thought. I fell asleep with my book in my hand and the light on. I didn't wake up until about four this morning.''

A quick wave of relief washed through him. ''I thought it was probably something like that. I saw your light on as I was going back to my cabin. I stopped and knocked on your door, but I didn't get an answer.''

He picked up the bottle of sunscreen lotion. ''If you turn over, I'll get your back for you.'' He uncapped the bottle as she turned onto her stomach. He tried to sound as if he were making casual conversation while rubbing the lotion on her skin. ''I've been thinking about taking some time off when the summer season is over, maybe taking a vacation. I've never been to Chicago. Do you think you could find some time to show me around town?'' He found himself holding his breath as he waited for her reaction to his overture.

Lexi raised up on one elbow and twisted around so she could see him. His words had come as a complete surprise. She searched his face for the honesty she hoped she would find there. Her pleasure and enthusiasm crept into her voice. A spontaneous smile emerged. ''Are you serious? Do you really think you could come to Chicago for a visit? That would be terrific. I'd love to show you around.''

Then some other words came back to her. Gloria had commented that Nick worked too hard and hadn't taken a real vacation since the dude ranch opened for business. Did that also include a one-week stay in Hawaii about six years ago? She stretched out on her stomach on the chaise longue so he couldn't see the concern she knew had suddenly clouded her features.

She had made her decision about what to do and had set the wheels in motion. Now she would have to live with the consequences of that decision. He was talking about traveling to Chicago to see her, but would he feel the same way in a couple of days after her mother arrived with Jimmy? Her inner struggle sent another chill through her in spite of the warm sun. She could feel the pressure mounting and the stress building inside her. She fought off the sadness that tried to gain a foothold.

He resumed massaging of her back and shoulders after applying more lotion. "I think I could work a trip to Chicago into my schedule." He leaned forward and whispered in her ear, "In fact, I would like that very much," then placed a soft kiss on her cheek.

His own words surprised him. The thought of taking off a few days and going to Chicago had not even crystallized in his mind before it came out of his mouth. He had been wrestling with his growing confusion over exactly what Lexi meant to him. He had steadfastly denied the recurring thought that he might be too emotionally involved with her, a denial that rang hollow even in his own mind. The possibility had hit him full force the previous evening the first time he had glanced at the saloon door and felt the sharp stab of disappointment when she didn't appear. There were several single women in the Hoedown Saloon that night, some of whom had openly flirted with him, but he could only focus on Lexi Parker.

He attempted to rationalize the situation. He didn't have time in his life for a full-fledged affair, the type that could easily turn into a serious relationship leading inevitably to a commitment. He already had way too many responsibilities, but try as he might, he could not shake off what he knew in his heart to be true.

But what about Lexi? What were her feelings? What did she want? The bothersome notion that there was something wrong, that Lexi had a secret she wasn't sharing, continued to linger in the back of his mind like a ghost haunting his every move.

Dinner that evening turned into a family affair of sorts. Gloria was again the hostess for Lexi's table. Nick joined them for dessert, then the three of them remained in the dining room after the other guests departed for various evening activities.

Nick produced a bottle of cognac and poured each of them an after-dinner drink. "I'd like to propose a toast. Here's to two very lovely ladies...one who has always encouraged me in whatever path I chose—" he acknowledged Gloria "—and one I've only known for a few days but in that short amount of time has become very special to me." He smiled at Lexi as he captured her gaze with his own and held it to him. The warmth of the moment settled over him. His heart filled with the closeness he felt for Lexi, an emotional involvement he felt very strongly but couldn't quite identify.

Lexi felt the heat of embarrassment spread across her cheeks, but she was unable to break eye contact with him. A soft glow settled over her, emphasizing just how much she loved him. She wanted to say something special, something from her heart, but the only thing that came out of her mouth was a whispered "Thank you."

"That was lovely, Nicky." Gloria raised her glass in response to his toast, then sipped her drink.

Gloria had only eaten part of her dessert following dinner, claiming it was too rich for her. As the three of them sat and talked, she began to absentmindedly nibble at the rest of it until she had consumed the last bite.

A little while later, Gloria pushed back from the table, a slight frown wrinkling her forehead. "As much as I'm enjoying this, it's probably time for me to go back to my cabin. I'm a little tired. I think I'll read for a bit, then go to bed early."

Nick immediately jumped to his feet, his concern all too evident. "Are you okay, Mom?"

Gloria smiled reassuringly. "Of course I'm okay."

"Are you sure? You looked like you were in pain for a moment."

Her spontaneous laugh did as much to answer his concern as her words. "Just a little twinge telling me I had no business eating the rest of that dessert and then following it with that equally rich after-dinner drink." She stifled a yawn, then added, "I think I'd better call it a night before I fall asleep here in the dining room. Good night, Lexi. Nicky, I'll see you in the morning."

Lexi offered a warm smile. "Good night, Gloria."

"Good night, Mom."

Lexi caught Nick's worried expression as he watched Gloria leave the dining room. She could tell he had not been appeased by Gloria's explanation of the pained look that had darted across her face. Lexi reached out and touched his arm.

"Are you all right?"

"Huh? Oh…yes, I guess so." His entire manner seemed distracted and vague as he continued to stare in Gloria's direction.

"Nick? Are you sure everything is okay?"

He turned to face her, but she could tell his ready smile had been forced. "Yes, I'm fine. I was just a little concerned about Mom. She keeps insisting that she's fine, but

I'm not so sure..." His voice trailed off as he furrowed his brow in thought.

She tried to reassure him and calm his concerns. "Your mother strikes me as a very practical woman. I'm sure if she wasn't feeling well, she would tell you."

"Well...she's definitely a very practical woman." He again shot a worried glance toward the door, then returned his attention to Lexi. "I'm sure you're right." He took her hand and gave it a tug until she was on her feet. He turned his head toward the connecting door to the saloon as soft strains of a slow song reached his ears. He gestured toward the music and cocked his head. "Would you do me the honor of joining me for a dance?"

"I'd like that...very much." Just his touch, something as simple as his holding her hand, sent tremors of excitement through her body. They reinforced her deep feelings of love, but at the same time increased her fears of what the next couple of days would bring. She wanted to retire to her cabin to wrestle with her anxieties in private, but she could not break away from the charismatic spell he cast over her. She went with him, willingly allowing him to lead her next door and out onto the dance floor just as she would have willingly allowed him to lead her anywhere else.

They spent the next two hours dancing, lost in each other's arms and oblivious to the people around them. By the time they left the saloon, Lexi had almost managed to forget her feelings of foreboding and doubts about what the immediate future held. They strolled along the path hand in hand until they reached Nick's cabin.

As soon as they stepped inside, the phone began to ring. Nick didn't know whether to be irritated or concerned. "Damn. A phone call this time of night can't be anything good.'' He placed a tender kiss on her cheek and flashed a reassuring smile. ''I'll be right back.''

He grabbed the cordless phone. His tone of voice conveyed an impatience with the unknown caller. ''Nick Clayton.'' He listened for a moment. His body stiffened to attention. His face went ashen and his stern expression immediately changed to one of grave concern. ''I'll be right there.''

He turned to Lexi, his urgency telegraphing itself before any words came out of his mouth. ''It's Mom…I've got to go. Can you get back to your cabin okay?''

''Yes, of course. What's wrong? Is there something I can do to help?'' A hard thud settled in the pit of Lexi's stomach as the full implication of the emergency swept over her. ''Is Gloria okay?''

''I don't know. I think she's having chest pains.'' His gaze darted around the room, then lit on his car keys. ''I'm afraid it might be…'' He didn't finish the thought. His deep concern showed in the focused concentration of his face. A sick feeling churned inside Lexi. Her timing couldn't have been worse. Tonight Nick was beside himself with worry about his mother, and there was no telling what turn Gloria's condition would take. The day after tomorrow he was going to meet Jimmy—the boy who might be his son.

Seven

Nick pulled his Ford Explorer into the parking lot at the hospital emergency room. He turned to Gloria and tucked the blanket around her shoulders. "You sit here and don't move. I'll get someone."

Gloria wiggled her arm out from beneath the blanket. "I'm okay, Nicky. It's only a little bit of indigestion. All this fuss is a waste of time and energy. There are sick people who need medical attention and I shouldn't be taking it away from them."

His voice and manner took on an air of absolute authority. "Sit here and don't move. We'll let a doctor decide if that's all it is."

Nick ran into the emergency room and returned a couple of minutes later with an orderly. They quickly and efficiently transferred Gloria to a wheelchair and took her inside. Nick started giving pertinent information to the clerk on duty while the orderly wheeled Gloria to a treatment room.

Nick paced up and down the waiting room, the tension inside him building to an uncomfortable level. As many times as Gloria had told him she was all right was as often as he had worried about her health. He glanced toward the treatment room every few minutes. A myriad of thoughts swirled around in his head. He hadn't been this distraught since the night his father died.

"How's Mom?"

Nick looked up at the sound of Danny's voice and saw him hurrying across the waiting room. "I don't know." He glanced toward the treatment room again. "I'm still waiting for word from the doctor."

"What happened? I was over by the stables showing this nice young lady around the grounds when Ken grabbed me and said you'd taken Mom to the emergency room."

"She called me...said she thought she was having a touch of indigestion from eating too much rich dessert...wanted me to bring her something to ease the discomfort." He glanced toward the treatment room again as he tried to split his attention between talking to Danny and watching for the doctor. "When I got to her cabin, she seemed to be having chest pains, so I packed her up and brought her here over her very vocal objections."

Danny rolled his eyes as he nodded his head. "Yep, I can just hear her insisting that she's fine and you telling her she's not."

Nick tried to get his mind on other things. "So...you were showing some nice young lady the grounds. A new arrival or someone I might have met?"

Danny grinned at him, his expression saying far more than his words. "The way you've been hovering around

Lexi, I didn't think you'd have time to notice anyone new. How's your romance doing?''

Nick snapped out the words. ''It's not a romance.'' He heard the irritation that had crept unwittingly into his voice, an irritation born from suddenly finding himself on the defensive. He forced a lid on his emotions and tried to find an inner calm. ''Lexi is…'' He glanced at the floor and emitted an audible sigh. ''Well, it doesn't matter. There's no way I can entertain any thoughts of a relationship with Mom's health being bad. And there's the business. Too many people are already depending on me— you, Mom, our employees and their families. I don't have room in my life for any more responsibilities than I already have. If Mom becomes more incapacitated, it would only add to that load.'' Nick glanced at the treatment room door again, then returned his attention to Danny. ''How can I possibly take on anything else knowing there's no way I can give it my total commitment?''

The moment of silence was interrupted by the arrival of the doctor. ''Mr. Clayton?''

''Yes, I'm Nick Clayton. This is my brother, Danny. How's Mom?''

''She's just fine, Mr. Clayton. It appears to be a simple case of indigestion. She says she ate too much of a rich dessert even though she knew it was going to disagree with her. However, I would like to keep her here overnight.''

''You're admitting her to the hospital? I thought you said she was all right.''

''It's just as a precaution. I can send her home if she insists, but I'd rather keep her for observation.''

Nick narrowed his eyes and studied the doctor for a moment. ''Are you sure that's all it is?''

The doctor gave him a confident smile. ''I'm sure, Mr.

Clayton. I'll contact her doctor—'' he glanced at the clipboard in his hand ''—Dr. Blanchard, first thing in the morning to apprise him of the situation. He may choose to stop by to see her, but I don't see any reason why we can't release her in the morning.''

Nick concluded his business with the emergency-room clerk, making sure all the insurance information was in place. He drove back to the ranch with Danny following right behind him.

He kept playing the words over and over in his mind. *How can I possibly take on anything else knowing there's no way I can give it my total commitment?* The more thought he gave to a relationship—a serious relationship—with Lexi, the more he liked the idea. He shook his head. He found himself in an uncomfortable situation and didn't know what to do about it. Lexi would be leaving after her vacation was over. He had to do something. He had suggested that he might take a few days off and go to Chicago, but then what?

He had never been afraid of anything other than showing weakness or appearing vulnerable in front of those who depended on him, and that number seemed to increase with each passing day. He'd tried new things without fear for his physical well-being. He'd tackled problems fully confident that he would be able to resolve them.

He couldn't say that anymore. Lexi Parker scared him. Or more accurately, what he felt and thought, the confusing emotions she aroused in him, scared him. He started to go to his cabin, but at the last minute detoured to Lexi's. Her light was on. He knocked softly at the door and she immediately opened it. He took her hand and stepped inside, closing the door behind him. Just her touch, the feel of her hand in his, provided instant comfort for his distress.

"How's Gloria?" Her concern showed in her eyes. "Is she okay?"

"Yes, she's fine. They're keeping her overnight for observation, but the doctor said there's nothing to worry about."

He brought her hand to his lips and kissed her palm. There was a strength about her that he needed at that moment, a comfort that he drew from her. He had never been in the position before where he *needed* emotional support from someone else. He had always been the one to lend his strength to others. Accepting it from someone else was new to him.

"I...uh...was afraid she might have had a heart attack." He had been terrified to say those words out loud for fear they might be true, but being with Lexi gave him the courage to verbalize that fear. "The doctor assured me that it was only a touch of indigestion—too much rich dessert."

She emitted a sigh of relief followed by a soft smile. "I'm glad to hear that. I've been worried."

He pulled her into his embrace and held her tightly against his body. He threaded his fingers through the silky strands of her hair and cradled her head against his shoulder. It felt so reassuring to have her in his arms, to be able to openly share his concerns and fears with someone, to touch her, to feel her breathing. It was a sensation he did not want to lose—to be able to show vulnerability without fear that it would be mistaken for weakness—but he didn't know what to do to keep it.

Too many responsibilities. Too many commitments. He felt the weight of it all descend on his shoulders again. He continued to hold her close, to revel in the intimacy. There were times when he envied Danny's ability to shrug off things he didn't want to deal with, and this was one of those times. He tried to shove the doubts away, to regain the confidence he had always been able to call on in times of stress, but he wasn't having much luck.

"Are you okay, Nick?" She slipped her arms around his waist. A shudder swept through her when she felt the tension in his body and his tautly drawn muscles. "You're tied up in knots." She couldn't imagine what had caused it. She looked up at him but wasn't quite sure what she saw on his face—exhaustion or trepidation. Then a panicked thought hit her and carried over to her voice. "Gloria is going to be all right, isn't she? You wouldn't lie to me, would you?"

He loosened his hold on her but did not release her from his embrace. He couldn't let go of the comfort she provided. He placed a tender kiss on her lips. "I'd never lie to you."

She closed her eyes and put her head against his shoulder. With all her heart she hoped it was the truth and applied to everything, not just Gloria's health. At the same time Lexi started to have a queasy feeling in her stomach when she admitted she'd been less than honest with him, but she managed to dismiss it as not being the same thing. After all, she had been trying to get at the truth. She hadn't lied to him; she had just not been forthcoming with the entire picture. It was different. So why did she suddenly feel as if she were being dishonest? Another layer to add to her ever-increasing feelings of guilt.

"Mom is just fine. I'm going to call her doctor in the morning just to double-check with him, but I'm sure she's okay. I guess I'm still a little tense, that's all. It's been a stressful couple of hours." He glanced toward the cabin door, then tugged on her hand. "Could I talk you into coming back to my cabin? I don't have my cell phone with me and I'd like to be near the phone…just in case."

"Sure." She offered up a reassuring smile, fully understanding his need to be with someone.

They walked hand in hand to Nick's cabin. Once inside, he poured each of them a glass of wine. He put his arm around her shoulders and drew her to him until they were snuggled into the corner of the couch. The remaining hours of the evening ticked away until well past midnight as each of them remained quietly absorbed in private thoughts.

Lexi's inner turmoil ripped through her, pulling her in two different directions. The stress and guilt that had become her constant companions escalated with each passing minute. Tomorrow and tomorrow night—that might be all the time she had left to spend with Nick. Her mother would arrive with Jimmy, then the entire world she had hoped would evolve as her future might crumble into dust instead. She closed her eyes in an effort to drive away the unpleasant possibility. Conflicting thoughts and feelings swirled around inside her until they converged into one confusing muddle. The one clear thing in her mind was her love for Nick Clayton.

It seemed like only moments later when Lexi heard the clock above the mantel chime twice. She tried to shake the fuzziness from her head. Two o'clock in the morning...she must have dozed off. Nick still had his arm around her, but he appeared to be asleep. The drawn lines on his face told her it was not a peaceful rest. As long as she stayed in his arms, she felt safe and secure. But how much longer would that last? The moment of truth that she had come to dread was almost upon her. She tried to ease herself off the couch without disturbing him.

He woke with a start, jerking to an upright position. His eyes darted around the living room as if he were trying to get his bearings, then his gaze landed on her. Softness settled over his face, easing the lines of tension. He smiled at her, then touched her cheek. He slid his fingers along her jawline, then cupped her chin in his hand. "I guess I'm not being a very good host, falling asleep like that."

"You weren't alone. I'm afraid I dozed off, too. I thought maybe I could leave quietly without disturbing you. I know you've had an exhausting day."

"Not so much so that you need to sneak out the door leaving me all alone on my couch." He captured her hand and pulled her down next to him. "Do you really need to rush off?"

She melted into his embrace again. She had no willpower where Nick was concerned. Her words came out as a soft whisper. "No, I don't need to leave."

"Good." He kissed her on the cheek, then snuggled up next to her in the corner of the couch.

He made no effort to initiate anything more intimate than the closeness they were already sharing. The warmth descended over her in a soft sensation that reinforced her feelings of love but did nothing to alleviate her anxiety. A confrontation loomed on the horizon, one she knew could not be avoided.

They remained on the couch, wrapped in each other's arms. She thought Nick had fallen asleep and she was afraid to move. She didn't want to disturb him again.

She knew—logically and intellectually—that she had done the right thing in instructing her mother to bring Jimmy to the ranch. So why were her insides tied in knots? Her temples throbbing with the onset of a headache? Her heart pounding with trepidation? She had once been so sure of everything, then she had not been sure of anything. Only the security of being wrapped in Nick's embrace kept her from panicking.

* * *

Danny looked up at the sound of the door. He immediately spotted Nick crossing the tack room. He held up the coffeepot toward him and cocked his head in a questioning manner. When Nick shook his head to indicate that he didn't want any, Danny filled his own mug and placed the empty pot in the sink. "What time is Mom being released from the hospital?"

"I just got off the phone with Dr. Blanchard. They'll be releasing her in about an hour. I have a couple of things to do, then I'm going over to get her."

"Did the doctor have anything new to add when you talked to him…something in addition to what the emergency-room doctor told us last night?"

Nick furrowed his brow as if turning something over in his mind. "No…he concurred with last night's diagnosis of simple indigestion. He says she's perfectly healthy and there's nothing to worry about."

Danny leaned back against the counter and took a swallow from his mug as he regarded his brother. "He's been saying that ever since she recovered from the car wreck. You're the only one who doesn't seem to realize it."

Nick shot Danny a sharp look. "Meaning…?"

"Nothing…it was just an observation." Danny set his coffee mug on the counter. "Do you want me to go with you to the hospital?"

"No, that won't be necessary. I'll be gone less than an hour. Mom will be home in time for lunch." He glanced at his watch. "I'd better get busy. I've still got a couple of things to finish before I go."

Nick left the tack room. His purposeful stride belied the inner doubts that clouded his thinking. Was he being overprotective of his mother? He had lost his father and almost lost his mother at the same time. She'd recovered from her life-threatening injuries but remained confined to a wheelchair. With his father gone, he had accepted the responsibilities of caretaker and protector for both his mother and his brother, a position he took very seriously.

He continued on toward his office, his confusion growing with each step he took. The gap between his entrenched sense of duty to his responsibilities on the one hand and on the other his personal desires where Lexi Parker was concerned continued to widen.

He spotted Lexi crossing the terrace. His spirits immediately brightened as he called out to her. "Lexi!"

She turned at the sound of her name and saw Nick hurrying in her direction. She'd had a busy morning. She hadn't expected to see Nick until after lunch and had hoped to get all her business handled before then. She had been awake most of the night. Her fears, anxieties, inner turmoil and a reignited sense of guilt combined to play havoc with her attempt to get some sleep. She had finally given up trying to guess what would happen after Jimmy's arrival.

It was with a heavy heart that she had returned to her cabin that morning. She tackled what she knew had to be done. She started to pack some of her clothes and prepare for the possibility that she might be leaving the next day. Then she had gone to the reservation desk to cancel her scheduled activities. It had been a difficult decision for her, but it was a reality she needed to face.

She smiled as Nick came to a halt next to her, trying her best to make it appear that nothing was amiss. "I thought you were going to the hospital this morning to get Gloria. Are you back already?"

"I'll be leaving in about half an hour or so. We'll be back before lunch. I'm having the chef fix something that we can have at my cabin rather than eating with the guests in the dining hall.'' He took her hand and gave it a gentle, loving squeeze. ''Would you like to join us?''

Her love for Nick welled inside her, momentarily pushing her worries into the background. Somehow everything would work out—it just had to. She returned his squeeze. ''I'd like that very much.''

''Good. I'll see you then.'' Nick reluctantly let go of her hand while his gaze lingered on her face. Then he turned and went to his office.

Nick quickly handled a few business matters, then drove to the hospital to pick up Gloria. After taking care of the paperwork, he drove her back to the ranch.

''I have lunch waiting in my cabin. Lexi will be joining us.''

A smile of pleasure lit up Gloria's face. ''I'm glad. She's a lovely young lady. I really like her.''

''And then after lunch I want you to get some rest.''

She drew in an exasperated breath, held it for a moment, then exhaled. ''What do you think I've been doing in the hospital, Nicky? Running a marathon? I'm as rested as I can get and I'm also perfectly fine. The emergency-room doctor pronounced me fit. It was only a little indigestion, just like I said. Dr. Blanchard says I'm in fine health. You seem to be the only one who doesn't understand that.''

A hint of irritation crept into her voice. ''You have to stop trying to be all things to all people. I've never encountered anyone with a more highly developed sense of responsibility, but it's way past time for you to start looking out for yourself. You can't spend the rest of your life putting everyone else's well-being above your own.''

''Now, Mom. I've got a nice lunch waiting. Why don't we concentrate on that?''

Her manner softened. ''You stepped in and took charge

after your father died. You held everything together at a time when we desperately needed someone with your strength and determination, but you're not the only person who's capable of handling problems.''

Nick squirmed uncomfortably. He had skirted this conversation with his mother on numerous occasions during the past year, but this time he didn't seem to be able to talk his way around it.

She cocked her head and leveled a serious gaze at him. ''Maybe you should spend less time worrying about me and the business and a little more time concentrating on Lexi.'' Having made her point, Gloria wheeled her chair toward Nick's cabin, leaving him standing in stunned silence.

How could he possibly think in terms of a serious relationship with Lexi when there were already too many demands on him now? There was no way he could ever make a commitment to something unless he was able to give it the attention and time it needed and deserved. He was being torn in two directions—what he wanted for himself and what was best for everyone else.

He hurried to catch up with Gloria. Just as they reached his cabin door, Lexi joined them.

She put her hand on Gloria's arm. ''It's good to see you. How are you feeling?''

''I feel terrific. Nick has, once again, made a big deal out of nothing. Right now, I'm looking forward to lunch. I was so pleased when Nick said you'd be joining us.''

Lunch turned out to be a delightful interlude. It was obvious to Lexi that there was nothing wrong with Gloria, just as she had claimed. Following lunch, Gloria insisted on going to work, leaving Lexi and Nick alone in his cabin.

His mother's words kept circulating through his mind

along with visions of what it would be like to wake up every morning with Lexi next to him. The concept filled him with warmth and began tipping the scales toward what he wanted from life.

He pulled Lexi into his arms, holding her in a loving embrace. Up until that moment, he had not clearly pictured all the possibilities that life could offer him. Things had been good. He had not needed to think beyond that. Until now. More and more his desires and needs encompassed the emotional link that Lexi provided. The thought scared him but the idea enthralled him.

His mouth found hers. It started as a soft kiss but quickly escalated into one of passionate intensity. He sought out the taste of her mouth, twining his tongue with hers. He caressed her shoulders, then allowed one hand to glide smoothly down her back until he cupped the roundness of her bottom. What had started as a desire for closeness had quickly turned into an all-consuming need.

"Lexi…"

He twined his fingers in her hair while cradling her head against his shoulder. He wanted to say something to let her know how he felt, but he couldn't put his feelings into the right words. So he contented himself with holding her a moment longer before releasing her from his embrace.

"I…uh…need to get to work. Will I see you this evening?" He wasn't happy with the hopeful tone that crept into his voice. It made him sound almost desperate for the answer he wanted to hear.

She smiled self-consciously, her gaze dropping to the floor. "Well, we'll all be eating in the dining hall, so I imagine so."

He cupped her chin in his hand and lifted her head until he could see into her eyes. "That's not exactly what I meant.'' The tightness pulled across his chest. He wanted to say so much but couldn't string the words together. ''Maybe an after-dinner stroll around the grounds? And then perhaps a quiet evening together?''

Every time he touched her, the same thing happened. Her insides melted and she turned to putty in his hands. She felt as if she could not catch her breath. To deny him was next to impossible. She smiled. ''I'd like that.''

His voice dropped to an intimate whisper. ''I'd like it, too.'' He placed a tender kiss on her lips. ''What are your plans for this afternoon? We have calf-roping lessons tomorrow. Would you like to get in some extra riding time so you'll be more comfortable with your horse? I'll have Ken set something up for you, if you'd like.''

His words caught her by surprise, then it dawned on her that he didn't know she had canceled the rest of her activities. The warmth his touch had caused suddenly turned cool as the realization of what would happen the next day came back to her. ''No...I think I'll go over to the pool for a while. I feel like a lazy afternoon.''

''I'll see you later, then.''

Lexi went to her cabin and Nick headed for the stables. She changed into her swimsuit, then went to the pool. Perhaps the heat of the sun would drive away the chill. But even as she settled into the lounge chair, she knew no amount of sunshine could lighten the task that awaited her the next morning when her mother and Jimmy arrived. She felt herself sinking further and further into the deception she had created, the lie born of necessity that had now turned on her to threaten her very existence.

Before the night was over, she would need to procure some information from Nick, something that would tell her she had chosen the right path. Or perhaps something to help ease her feelings of guilt. She closed her eyes. She loved him so much. Surely everything would work out. There just wasn't any way that the Nick Clayton she knew could possibly be the same man Marnie described.

A little shiver ran up her back. No matter how hard she tried to convince herself and how much she wanted it to be so, she could not quite make herself believe that everything would turn out okay.

Eight

Nick took Lexi's hand in his as they left the dining room following dinner. "It's a beautiful night. How about a walk out by the reflecting pond, then we can go back to my cabin? I have several movies on tape."

She forced a smile in an attempt to make it appear as if nothing was wrong. "That sounds lovely."

They walked along in silence for a few minutes. The tension started building inside her during dinner and now churned almost out of control. Knowing it was self-induced didn't help. She didn't know how much more of this sense of foreboding she could handle. She tried to ignore it and gather her thoughts together in some sort of logical manner. The last thing she wanted to do was sound as if she was giving him the third degree or prying into his personal life even though that was precisely what she was about to do—as soon as she screwed up her courage.

When they arrived at Nick's cabin, he showed her

where he kept his tapes, then went to the kitchen to get them some wine. She sat on the floor and stared at the selection of movies without really seeing the titles. Her mind was filled with what she knew would be the hardest thing she ever had to do.

"Did you find a movie you want to see?" Nick's voice filtered in from the kitchen, interrupting her gloomy train of thought.

"Uh...yes..." She grabbed a movie from the shelf without even bothering to look at the title.

"Go ahead and pop it into the VCR. I'll be there in a minute."

Lexi turned her attention to the tape she had grabbed, finally noting the title. She'd seen the movie when it was first released. It was the story of a woman's family who tried to find the father of her child after she'd been killed. In the movie, the man was the real father and had abandoned her before the child was born. Under his charming manner lurked a cold, unfeeling man who thought only of himself. Would this turn out to be life imitating art? It was a thought she couldn't bear to accept. She squeezed her eyes shut as she tried to find a bit of calm in the storm that seemed to be gathering momentum.

"Here." Nick handed her a glass of wine. "Come on, let's sit on the couch." He picked up the remote control and clicked on the television and VCR. "Which movie did you select?"

She handed him the tape without saying anything. He glanced at the title, then put it in the VCR and started it. He didn't show any visible reaction to the subject matter of the movie. Perhaps fate had decided to give her a break. She had randomly chosen a movie that would allow her to open the topic of conversation without it appearing to have sprung out of the blue.

The comfort of his arm around her shoulders helped ease some of her anxiety as she settled onto the couch. She agonized over exactly how to introduce the subject so that it sounded casual. She nervously cleared her throat, then forged ahead. "That's an…uh…interesting premise for a movie. What do you think about that?"

He shifted his weight so that he could get a better look at her, a confused expression on his face. "Think about what?"

"About a woman having a child out of wedlock." Maybe if she took it one step at a time, it wouldn't seem so suspicious.

"It's hardly an unusual happening."

"I mean, do you think a child should have a father around while he—or she—is growing up? That there should be two parents to raise that child?"

"I think it's always a shame when a family breaks up, but I think there are times when it's better for the child to be raised by one loving parent rather than in a home where both parents are constantly fighting and imposing their battles on that child."

Her frustration grew. She fought to keep it hidden. She obviously wasn't getting her point across. Was her question too obscure for him to get what she was really asking? She clenched her jaw for a second as another thought occurred to her. Perhaps he was being purposely obtuse. She tried again. "I guess we're getting away from my original question, which was about a woman having a child out of wedlock and no father anywhere on the scene rather than a family breaking up later."

She inwardly flinched when she heard the edge that crept into her voice, a telling sign that it was more than just an idle question brought on by the content of the movie. She studied his reaction, hoping that he had not noticed. A flicker of something darted across his features, but it disappeared too quickly for her to read it.

Nick tried to keep his confusion from showing as he wondered how to answer her question—a question he didn't understand. Was he just being dense or was she trying in a roundabout way to tell him something? To get his reaction to a subject before committing herself to saying anything specific? Had she purposely selected that movie as a means of opening a topic of conversation? He found the entire thing baffling.

He tried to stall for time in an attempt to figure out how to handle this surprise twist to the evening and the even stranger twist to the conversation. He adopted a light outer manner and tone to his voice in an attempt to show that he thought she was joking. He chuckled softly. "Now why in the world would you ask such an odd question?"

A trickle of panic began to set in. Had she gone too far or had she been too blunt? It was too late to retract her questions. She tried to contain a nervous laugh without much success. "It was just idle curiosity, that's all." She made a gesture toward the television, hoping she'd appear casual and offhand. "Probably a thought brought on by the movie. But since I've already asked the question—" her anxiety increased along with the churning in her stomach "—I'd be interested in your answer." She swallowed down the rising panic as she waited for his response.

"Well…as I said, single-parent families are a pretty common thing in today's society."

She saw the confusion in his features, but she also saw the wariness in his eyes. It sent a nervous tremor through her body. She forced out the words, the question she really wanted answered. "What about a man who fathers a child, then refuses to take responsibility?"

"That's certainly a loaded question." He smiled self-consciously as his mind went into double time trying to figure out what was going on. Could all of this have something to do with her initial attitude when she first arrived at the ranch? With the way she seemed to vacillate between being open and then being standoffish? But what could that possibly have to do with him? Then a light finally penetrated the fog that surrounded his thoughts.

She had been trying to tell him something important and he had been too dense to realize it. He berated himself for being so thick-skulled and slow to catch on. She wanted him to know that she had a child even though she had never been married. And even more important, that the child's father had abandoned her when he found out she was pregnant. The entire situation left him feeling oddly unsettled. He saw the anxiety on her face and knew he had to provide her with an answer to her question. He took a calming breath, then did his best to respond as honestly as he could.

"A man who would father a child, then refuse to accept any responsibility does not deserve to be called a man." He hoped his answer would satisfy her until he could figure out what was going on. His first instinct was to handle it the same way he handled any situation—to take the direct approach and just ask her if she was talking about herself. He dismissed the idea as quickly as it had materialized. If she wanted him to know, she would have told him outright rather than taking this strangely circuitous route.

He pretended to be watching the movie, but it was a far cry from where his attention rested. There were too many things up in the air, too many problems that didn't seem to have any easy answers. He felt as if he were treading on thin ice and needed to be very careful about what moves he made. He pulled her closer to him and stared at the television as the doubts and worries circulated through his mind.

The one concrete reality was Lexi sitting next to him and the very real and deep feelings he had for her—feelings that he desperately needed to put into some kind of understandable form. He wrapped both arms around her, maneuvering her onto his lap as he pressed his lips tenderly against her forehead. He didn't understand what was going on and he wasn't clear about what he wanted in the long run, but for now. Lexi dominated his thoughts.

Once again, Lexi felt safe and protected in his embrace. His answer had given her hope. By his own admission, he would never have abandoned Marnie and Jimmy. She believed what he said. Her spirits perked up until a nagging thought dashed them. He might not know he had a son. Marnie might not have told Nick about the pregnancy. Perhaps her lie was not who Jimmy's father was, but whether he knew it.

Her moment of elation was short-lived. The matter had not been resolved yet. Lexi still needed to determine whether or not Nick and Marnie were having an affair at the time Marnie was in Hawaii, which would make Nick Jimmy's father even if he had not been aware of it. Time was running out. Her mother would be arriving with Jimmy late the next morning. She snuggled closer and put her head against his shoulder. Right now it was enough that he vindicated her belief that he would never have deserted a woman carrying his child.

She could feel the strong beat of his heart and the even rhythm of his breathing. The idea of being able to spend all her evenings enveloped in his arms appealed to her very much. It felt so right. She loved him. She didn't know how it could have happened so quickly, but it had. Everything simply had to turn out all right.

He shifted his weight on the couch, startling her out of her reverie. She looked up at him, and a moment later his mouth was on hers. He enveloped her with the heat of his desire, sending a wave of incendiary passion through her body and leaving no doubt as to his intentions for the rest of the evening.

Lexi reached her arms around his neck and ran her fingers through his thick hair. She responded to his fervor with a euphoric elation of her own, one that rose from the deepest well of her emotions. If this was to be her last night with Nick, then let it be one that would live in her memory for the rest of her life.

The noise from the television ceased to exist. The movie that she had not really been watching disappeared from her consciousness. All she wanted, everything that mattered to her at that precise moment, revolved around Nick Clayton and how much she loved him. A soft moan escaped her throat as he brushed his tongue against hers. She surrendered totally to his control.

Her taste was addictive to him. He wanted more and more. He wanted it all. He ignored his unsettled feelings about exactly what their relationship was, where it was headed, and Lexi's odd conversation. She was everything he needed. She filled a void in his life that he hadn't even known existed before they made love the first time. Since that night, she had occupied his every waking moment and also invaded his dreams. His mother's words about tending to his own life and putting himself first for a change floated around in his mind, but they refused to settle anywhere.

He broke off the kiss just long enough to stand up. He tugged at her hand. His words came out in a husky whisper. "Come to bed with me." He kissed the palm of her hand. "I want to make love to you all night long."

She rose from the couch, her voice filled with as much passion as his. "Yes." She went with him willingly, even eagerly.

It took only a couple of minutes for their clothes to be deposited on the floor and the covers on the bed to be turned back.

Nick scooped her up in his arms and gently placed her in the middle of the bed. He took a moment to rake his gaze over her body. Her dusky pink nipples had already formed into taut peaks. The fires of desire burned in the depths of her eyes. Her golden hair flowed across the pillow. He felt hard bands tighten across his chest, restricting his already labored breathing. Just the thought of making love to her excited him more than anything else ever had.

He stretched out on the bed next to her, running his foot along the curve of her calf. He captured her mouth in a fervent kiss, this time with an aggression that clearly spoke of unbridled passion and intense longing.

He threaded his fingers through her silky hair as he smothered her face with kisses. His skin tingled everywhere she touched him, culminating in a heated rush when she stroked his rigid manhood. He inhaled her fragrance, devoured her taste and reveled in how good she felt in his arms. No one...not even if he lived to be a thousand years old...could ever excite him the way she did.

He trailed the tip of his tongue from the base of her throat down to the valley between her breasts. He seductively drew her puckered nipple into his mouth, holding it there for a moment as he teased the bud with his tongue. He suckled, at first softly, then with increased ardor. He wanted to devour all of her, to consume her very essence in a way that would allow him to keep it forever.

He moved to her other nipple and captured it with equal ardor. He felt her breathing as the vitality of her existence radiated to him. He ran his hand up her inner thigh, until he reached the moist heat of her sex.

He heard a quick gasp followed by her moan of pure pleasure when he slipped his finger between her feminine folds. She closed her fingers around his rigid manhood. He shuddered when she stroked and caressed his need.

He kissed the underside of each breast, then trailed little kisses across her stomach and down her abdomen. His breath whispered through the feathery softness covering her most private place. He felt her entire body tense and her cry of ecstasy when his mouth found the hot core of her womanhood.

He felt the tremor start deep inside her body, then spread out, a provocative sensation that further fueled his already highly aroused condition even more. He wanted to tell her about his feelings, but once again he couldn't clearly define them or put them into words. He kissed his way back up to her breasts, then rolled over on his back, taking her with him. He wrapped his arms around her body and held her close.

His whispered words were thick with the weight of his passion. "I want to make love to you over and over again...all night long."

Her response matched his in its intensity. "Me, too."

He grasped her hips, lifted, then lowered her onto his hardness. The magnitude of the emotion that washed over him at the moment of their joining was greater than anything he had ever known. There was far more at stake here than the heated intensity of two people making love. No man could ever want or need more than what he experienced when they were together. It far exceeded the physical passions they shared. Somewhere in the back of his mind he knew there was a word for what was happening between them, something that could explain the way he felt. For a brief moment the word love tried to push its way into his consciousness, but all it produced was a rush of panic that quickly shoved it from his thoughts. But the word refused to be dismissed. It continued to linger in the deep recesses of his mind.

He rolled her body over with his, being careful not to break the tangible connection that physically bound them together. He set a slow rhythm, wanting the pure bliss of the moment to last as long as possible…maybe even a lifetime.

She wrapped her arms and legs around him. Her hips rose and fell to match his movements. The pace quickened, each of them lost in the throes of passion as they drew nearer and nearer to the moment of ultimate release.

The convulsions started deep inside her. They swept through her body, quickly engulfing her on every level of her existence. She clung tightly to Nick. Her pulse raced almost out of control. She had never been transported to such heights of rapture. No one had ever filled her with the total and complete ecstasy that engulfed her at that moment. And she knew no one else ever would.

Hard spasms coursed through Nick's body. He tightened his hold on Lexi, embracing her as if she were the very essence of life itself—the reason for his existence. He continued to hold her until the spasms had subsided and his breathing returned to near normal. He raised himself up on one elbow and gazed into her sparkling eyes.

A thin sheen of perspiration covered her face. He brushed an errant lock of hair away from her damp cheek, then placed a loving kiss on her lips. He wanted very much to please her, to be sure that her needs were taken care of. His words were soft, the strong emotions living inside him clinging to them as he spoke. "Is there anything you want…or need? Can I get anything for you?"

She knew what he meant, but her thoughts went in a different direction. Was there anything she wanted? Only to have the questions resolved about Jimmy's father and Marnie's relationship with Nick...to know for a fact that he'd had no involvement with her sister. And then to be able to forge a lifetime bond with him. She returned her attention to his question as she reached up and touched her fingertips to his cheek. "I can't think of a thing that could improve on this."

He settled back into the softness of the bed, holding her close to him. He stroked her hair as he cradled her in his arms. She again felt warm and protected, but the sensation was a bittersweet feeling. Her entire world could come crashing down around her in the morning when her mother arrived with Jimmy. If it were only her own involvement, the matter would be closed. She knew in her heart that Nick could never be guilty of abandoning Marnie knowing she was carrying his child, or deserting that child after it was born.

Unfortunately, the matter was complicated by the existence of a five-year-old boy whose future was at stake.

She rested her head against his chest and slipped her arm around his waist. A tremor of apprehension shivered its way through her body. She drew in a quavering breath. Unbridled joy turned to sadness. She closed her eyes, trying to calm her anxiety, but the tremors refused to be stilled. She placed a soft kiss on his chest. Everything had to work out...it just had to. She tried unsuccessfully to suppress a sigh.

Nick felt the tremor in her body, then heard her sigh. Her words and her reactions didn't match. She said things were fine, but her body told a different story. Things were far from being fine. He sensed a reserve about her as it she were pulling away. He didn't understand it. And it frightened him.

Everything about the past few days frightened him. He had finally accepted his mother's overnight stay in the hospital as being exactly what two doctors and Gloria had told him it was—a simple case of indigestion and nothing to worry about. But that did not lessen the long list of responsibilities that rested heavily on his shoulders.

It was his job to make sure Gloria's future was secure and that his kid brother had a steadying hand to keep him from doing anything too frivolous with the family business. And then there was the business itself. The Via Verde Dude Ranch employed over one hundred people who depended on him to provide income for their families. Somehow he had to find a way to make it all work. He had to redefine his responsibilities and open up his life. He needed to find an ongoing place in his life for Lexi.

Nick was truly torn between his responsibilities and his personal desires. He needed to clearly define his relationship with Lexi. But there was more to it than that. If his suspicions were correct, there was also a child who needed to be figured into that equation. The dilemma ripped through his consciousness, leaving him more confused than ever. He held Lexi close, not knowing what else to do. He remained silent as he continued to wrestle with the quandary.

Even the comfort of Nick's arms could not dilute the feelings of guilt that flooded over Lexi to the point where she feared she might drown in them. She felt as if she were literally fighting to survive. Her loyalties, everything she had always believed in, had been shattered by her intimate involvement with the man Marnie had professed to be the father of her son...the same man Lexi had fallen head over heels in love with. And the worst was yet to come.

She knew she needed to prepare him for her mother's arrival at the ranch. She nervously cleared her throat, then stammered out her words. "My...uh...mother will be arriving tomorrow. She'll be staying for a couple of days."

"Really? I don't recall you mentioning it before. Do you want me to check and see if there's a larger cabin available since there'll be two of you?"

Three of us, she thought. "No, if I could just get a rollaway bed, that will be fine. Do I notify housekeeping about that? And about some more towels for the bathroom?"

"I can take care of that for you if you like." He placed a tender kiss on her forehead.

"No." She had spoken too quickly. She slowed her response in an attempt to sound casual. "Thank you, but I can handle it. I don't want you to use your time running around doing little favors for me when you have far more important things to do."

"It's really no bother. Was this a sudden decision on her part to join you for a couple of days?"

"Well, no...we had talked about the possibility, if she could get away..." Deeper and deeper—she had to stop edging around the truth before she buried herself completely under her deception.

Nick released her from his embrace and propped himself up on one elbow as he gave her a searching look. "You sound like you're more troubled by her visit than you're pleased. Is there a problem of some sort?"

"No...uh, well...there is...umm...something we have to talk about, a matter that needs discussing and..."

He furrowed his brow in confusion. "Your mother is coming here so the two of you can discuss something?"

"No…" She hesitated, not sure how to go about correcting his assumption. "I mean, something that you and I need to—"

"Then there *is* something wrong." His words came out with a sense of urgency. He brushed a kiss across her lips. "Tell me what it is."

She heard the concern in his voice and it tore her up inside. Pain and turmoil filled her to the point where there was almost no room left. How could she go on deceiving him like this? She suddenly felt cheap and dishonest, certainly not someone deserving of his concern and caring. She berated herself for having said anything and for letting her uneasiness show, but it was too late. "No, not now. We can discuss it tomorrow, after my mother arrives." She finally forced her gaze to meet his. "Could you set aside some time tomorrow to be alone with me so we can talk?"

He gave her a puzzled look. "Sure, if that's what you want. Just let me know when." He studied her for a moment—the distress etched into her features, the anxiety in her eyes and the nervousness that seemed to be controlling her. He didn't like it. Something was wrong and he wanted to know what it was, but he didn't know how to go about getting her to tell him.

Whatever had been bothering her was apparently about to be brought out into the open. He held her closely, trying to let her know that everything would be all right, but not knowing how to put it into words. Whatever had her so upset could be resolved if they worked it out together, but what in the world could it be that required privacy yet couldn't be discussed in the bedroom? A feeling of helplessness rose inside him. There should be something he could do, but he didn't know what. He was a man accustomed to being in control, or at least being in charge.

Suddenly, he found himself in the position of being neither and he didn't like it.

His voice conveyed reassurance and an outward show
of strength even though it was a far cry from the way he
felt. ''We can work this out, Lexi, whatever it is that's
bothering you. Nothing is as terrifying or bothersome
when you bring it out into the open and share it with
someone—'' he brushed a kiss against her lips ''—like
me. We'll work together and find a way to resolve it. Are
you sure you don't want to talk about it now?'' He gave
a little chuckle in an attempt to put her at ease and also
break the nearly unbearable tension building inside him.
''I can't imagine a place or time more private than what
we have right now.''

''Not now...not tonight. It will have to wait until tomorrow.'' Lexi closed her eyes and tried to take comfort
from his words. With all her heart, she hoped he was right,
that they could resolve everything. Then she could finally
put Marnie's accusations to rest and feel she had fulfilled
her obligation.

Guilt and anxiety still wound their way through her.
The feeling of foreboding grew stronger. She didn't know
which way to turn or what to do that would be any different from the path she had chosen. Rightly or wrongly,
she had to see this through to the end. A quick shudder
shook her body. She only hoped that end would not lead
to disaster.

There was one thing she was certain of, though. She
knew she could not spend the entire night with Nick in
his bed and in his arms. She could not continue to per-
petuate the situation she had created or live with the deceit
she had brought to his bed. Somehow she needed to steel
herself against the love she felt for this man. Jimmy's

future had to come first. She must put some distance between herself and this far-too-tempting man.

Lexi stirred uneasily, finally managing to ease herself out of Nick's embrace. She sat up and ran her fingers through her long hair in an effort to smooth it away from her face. "I…I think it would be better if I went back to my cabin tonight." She felt his muscles tense as he enfolded her in his embrace again. She finally managed to wiggle free of his hold only to have him pull her back into the comfort of the bed.

"Why?"

"I…I have several things that I need to do before my mother arrives. I think it would just be better if I went back to my cabin now rather than in the morning."

He kissed a spot behind her ear, then dropped his voice to a soft, seductive level that sent a new ripple of desire through her body. "The shuttle from the airport won't be here until ten-thirty in the morning. You'll have lots of time to do whatever you need to do before your mother arrives."

She slipped out of the bed before he had an opportunity to coax her back under the covers. There wasn't anything she would rather do than stay with him, snuggled into the warmth and security of his arms, but she knew she had to be strong where her conscience dictated. She rallied her determination, then reached for her clothes while carefully avoiding eye contact with him.

"I think it really would be better if I went back to my cabin now. I'm sure you have a busy day tomorrow and could probably use a good night's sleep." It felt as if her insides had been rendered into tatters. She pulled on her clothes as quickly as she could.

Nick reached for her hand, grabbing it before she could step out of his reach. He slid out of bed, a worried expression on his face and deep concern in his voice. "I don't understand what's going on here, Lexi. It seems like you can't get out the door quick enough."

She finally looked up into the clear blue honesty of his eyes. Emotion gripped her so tightly that she wanted to cry. She saw his bewilderment and it added yet another layer of guilt to her already unbearable load.

He placed his fingertips beneath her chin and lifted her head until he could look into her eyes as she silently pleaded for his understanding and patience. He pulled her into his arms, his heavy sigh of resignation saying he would let her handle it her own way. "Could you at least wait long enough for me to put on some clothes so I can walk you back to your cabin?"

She forced a tiny smile. "Yes…thank you. That would be nice." She rapidly progressed from apprehension to a full-blown fear of what the next day would bring. She dreaded what she knew she could not change. If only she could turn back the clock and handle everything differently, but it was too late for that. She had no options other than to continue with the plan she had already set in motion.

Nick pulled on sweatpants and a T-shirt, then stuck his feet into a pair of sneakers. He folded her into his embrace again as he brushed a soft kiss on her mouth. "Are you sure you won't change your mind?"

"I can't." Her voice was a mere whisper, her words barely audible. Even with his arms wrapped around her, she felt horribly alone.

Nine

Nick stood at his office window, staring out at the front drive. He watched as the shuttle van from the airport pulled up in front of the registration lobby. He had spent a miserable night, tossing and turning without getting much sleep. Things had gone from bad to worse. He didn't understand what had happened, why Lexi seemed so upset about her mother's visit and why she had insisted on returning to her own cabin. There had to be something he could have done, but he didn't know what.

He spotted her walking from the lobby to the van. There was a stiffness to her movements, a reluctance that said she was not all that anxious to greet her arriving guest. A ray of hope tried to find its way into his thinking. Was it possible that her odd behavior had nothing to do with a problem between them? Could it be the result of an ongoing estrangement between her and her mother?

Nothing more than nerves over an attempt to patch things up?

He desperately wanted to rush across the terrace, pull her into his arms and do whatever he needed to do to make everything all right. He wanted her to be happy, but he didn't know how to make it happen. Nick Clayton—the man who took care of everything and everyone—had never felt so lost.

He spotted the woman in her mid-fifties as soon as she stepped out of the van. A definite family resemblance told him she must be Lexi's mother. A moment later, a cold chill passed through his body. A little boy—he appeared to be about five years old—came bounding out of the van and ran to Lexi. She greeted him with a big smile, then knelt and gave him a warm hug and a kiss on the cheek. The same family resemblance extended to him, too.

All of Nick's concerns, fears and curiosity—everything that had been churning inside him—had now been answered. This little boy must surely be her son. But why had she been so secretive and vague about it? Why couldn't she have just come out and told him she had a son? One thing resolved, but more questions brought to light. The situation had become more confused, not less.

He took a steadying breath and headed toward his office door. He didn't know if Lexi expected him to appear on the scene, but he intended to do just that. He quickly crossed the lobby and exited the building.

He watched Lexi and the little boy as he crossed the terrace. The obvious love and closeness between them overshadowed the concerns and anxieties that seemed to have guided her actions for the past couple of days. The radiant glow surrounding them sent an emotional jolt through him that touched his heart on the deepest level possible.

A troublesome thought pricked him, something he had never considered a problem...until now. He had not been around children very much and didn't know how to talk to them. He didn't have a clue what to do with them or about them. They made him uncomfortable. The Via Verde certainly had its share of children vacationing with their parents. In fact, they offered a wide variety of activities specifically designed for children. But that was one responsibility he had always managed to leave in the capable hands of others more suited to that task—like Danny.

A combination of anxiety and trepidation knotted in the pit of his stomach as he drew closer to Lexi and her family. A tremor of uncertainty shivered its way through his body when the little boy looked up and fixed an intense gaze on him. Then the boy grinned at him, showing a missing front tooth and dimples.

Lexi looked around to see what had captured Jimmy's attention and immediately spotted Nick closing in on them. A sinking feeling spread through her body. She wasn't sure exactly what to say. She hadn't anticipated a confrontation quite so soon. She tamped down her apprehension and rose to her feet. She glanced at her mother, noting the curious expression on her mother's face and the way her gaze darted between Lexi and Nick.

Nick extended his most charming host smile. "Hello, Lexi. I see your guests have arrived. Is there something I can do to help you get settled in?"

There was a second of awkward silence as Nick stood his ground, obviously waiting to be introduced. Lexi nervously cleared her throat. "Uh...yes. Nick, I'd like you to meet my mother, Colleen Parker. Mother, this is Nick Clayton. And this—" she put her arm affectionately around her nephew's shoulder "—is Jimmy."

Nick and Colleen exchanged polite greetings as Jimmy continued to stare up at Nick, fascination clearly etched on his little face. Lexi wasn't sure what to say or what to do. She heard the caution in Nick's voice and the reserve in her mother's tone. They couldn't all stand there and continue to stare at each other. The pressure was on her. She had to do something.

Jimmy finally resolved her dilemma by speaking up as he continued to stare at Nick. "Are you a real cowboy? With a horse and everything?"

There was something about the encounter—the open wide-eyed innocence and curiosity on the little boy's face—that struck Nick as surprisingly appealing. He stared at Jimmy, not at all sure how to respond to him.

He finally returned the little boy's grin and managed an answer. "Yep...I'm a real cowboy. I have a horse and a lasso and all that cowboy stuff."

The type of admiration and wonder usually reserved for idols and heroes surrounded Jimmy's words. "Gosh...really? Do you round up the cows like the cowboys do on television?"

"I sure do."

It was obvious that Jimmy was totally fascinated with Nick. "Can I see your horse?"

"Sure—" Nick nervously glanced in Lexi's direction "—if that is okay with everyone." He had already engaged in more conversation with Jimmy than he ever had with any other child. Even though he found this little boy endearing, he desperately wanted some time alone with Lexi. He needed to know why she had not told him about her son. He also knew he had to somehow sort out his feelings about what type of relationship he and Lexi had and where he wanted it to go. He now needed to add the new element of her son into the equation. One thing was clear to him—he didn't want her to disappear from his life when her vacation was over.

Lexi had closely followed the exchange between Jimmy and Nick. She saw the fascination and adoration on Jimmy's face as he looked up at Nick. She also saw the wariness on Nick's features but didn't know how to interpret it. Once again, apprehension churned in her stomach and tension throbbed at her temples.

All her plans had been to no avail. From the moment she had arrived at the ranch on the shuttle van, nothing had gone as she had anticipated it would. It seemed that everything had conspired against her, from her first attraction to a sexy cowboy who turned out to be Nick Clayton to the disturbing moment when Jimmy and Nick stared at each other with mutual curiosity.

Lexi knelt at Jimmy's side, pretending an enthusiasm that was a long way from what she felt. "Would you like to see the horses? Grandma can take you to the corral. Doesn't that sound like fun?"

Jimmy hugged her around the neck, his genuine enthusiasm showing in his voice. "Yeah. I'd like that." He looked over at Colleen. "Can we go now, Grandma?"

"Sure." Colleen smiled at him and took his hand.

Lexi rose and gave what she hoped would appear as a casual smile. She handed her mother a key. "I've already checked you in and I'll have them take your suitcase directly to the cabin. After looking at the horses, maybe Jimmy would like to play in the children's swimming pool."

Lexi watched as her mother took Jimmy, leaving her alone with Nick. The moment of truth had arrived. Her mouth went dry and her throat started to tighten up. She reached into her pocket to reassure herself that the postcards Marnie had sent from Hawaii were still there—the ones saying she and Nick were having a marvelous time.

The churning anxiety in her stomach turned into a sick feeling that tried to work its way up her throat. She had never been as fearful about what might happen as she was at that moment. She saw the questioning look on Nick's face and realized he was about to say something. She held up her hand to stop him.

"Before you say anything, I have to know something." She heard the quaver in her voice but didn't know how to make it go away. "I need to know where you were about six years ago."

"What?" His disbelief rang loud and clear in his voice. "I was right here, where I always am." He furrowed his brow in confusion and fixed her with a quizzical gaze. "That's when you said your sister was here and you asked if I remembered her. I looked her up in our old picture files and found a photograph of her. I told you I recalled her visit after I recognized her from the photograph."

She nervously cleared her throat. "No, not then. I mean three months later, uh, later than when my sister was here." The words spilled out of her mouth, but she didn't seem to be able to ask an intelligent question or put together an articulate sentence. She couldn't get her mind and her mouth to work together.

Nick stared at her with an expression of total bewilderment. "Three months *after* the time your sister was here?" He continued to stare at her as if racking his brain in an effort to come up with an answer to her question. Suddenly, his expression brightened as he remembered.

"I was in the hospital with a concussion, a broken leg and three cracked ribs along with assorted bruises and abrasions as a result of landing wrong when I was thrown from a horse." He cocked his head and fixed her with a questioning look. "What's so important about that? What difference does it make where I was?"

Had she heard him correctly? He was in the hospital? She expelled the breath she'd been holding while waiting for his response. It was a far cry from any of the possibilities she had considered. The weight that had been pressing on her chest began to lift. Then a sobering thought struck her. He could have been in the hospital in Hawaii, which would still place him with Marnie just as she had claimed. Lexi had to know. She had gone this far. One way or the other, she had to finish this now.

"What hospital were you in? Where?" She held her breath again while awaiting one more answer.

His confused expression darkened as it took on a look of irritation. His voice carried an edge to it. "The one about five miles down the road. I'll be happy to show you the medical bills if you need some sort of proof beyond my word. What's going on here, Lexi? Why would my broken bones be of interest to you, let alone somehow important?"

Lexi could not contain the audible sigh of relief or the joy she felt in her heart. Nick Clayton could not be Jimmy's father. There was no way he could have been in Hawaii with Marnie at the same time as he was in a hospital in Wyoming. She also felt sad and betrayed. All those years Marnie had lied to her, had lied to everyone. And Lexi didn't know why.

The oppressive weight finally lifted from her, leaving an overwhelming sense of relief that it was finally over. She had accomplished what she had set out to do…sort of. She had not found Jimmy's father, but she had determined that Nick Clayton was not that man. There was no reason to even mention any of this to him, to embarrass him by disclosing her sister's false accusations. She tried to ignore the sudden wave of apprehension that swept over her, a surge of trepidation that said she would not be able to walk away from the matter that easily. Would there be any purpose in simply blurting out her sister's accusations and risking a negative reaction? Or would it be better if she tried to quietly smooth things over and slowly ease her way into a conversation where she could reveal the truth to him? She didn't know what to do. She felt an ominous foreboding—she had to do something, she had to somehow find a way to explain everything to Nick before it was too late. But for now she needed to get away from him, to find a place where she could think out the problem and come up with a way to approach what she now realized would be a very delicate situation.

She mustered as much outer composure as she could, took his hand and gave it a little squeeze. "Well, I'd better see how Mother and Jimmy are getting along. I'll see you later."

Her words caught him by surprise. "Wait a minute." Nick was not sure exactly what had just happened. "You can't run off just like that." He had not anticipated her leaving during what he considered an unfinished conversation. What did his broken bones and a hospital stay have to do with anything? And why did she suddenly seem so relieved and pleased with the information? Whatever had been going on was not over as far as he was concerned. He intended to ask some straighforward questions and wanted answers.

She glanced toward the corral where her mother and Jimmy were, then back at Nick. He saw the wariness in her eyes, something that seemed to almost border on panic. Her voice lacked the confidence that was there just a few minutes earlier. "I think I'd better go. Mother looks like she's ready to find the cabin so Jimmy can change and go to the pool.''

Lexi hurried toward the corral before he had a chance to say anything more. A sinking sensation worked its way through his consciousness, leaving him decidedly uneasy in his thoughts and feelings. The little boy had called Lexi's mother Grandma. That confirmed it in his mind—Jimmy was her son, just as he had suspected. She had tried to tell him in a roundabout way, asking him what he thought about a woman having a child out of wedlock. But why had she made arrangements for her mother to bring the little boy here rather than just coming out and telling him? Had she made an assumption about what their future relationship would be? One thing was for certain—whatever the future held for them would now include this little boy.

Nick turned and slowly walked toward his office, his mind totally occupied with a new set of concerns. He entered the lobby and walked past the registration desk, acknowledging the desk clerk's attempt to get his attention but waving his hand to indicate he didn't have time to stop. He continued on down the hallway to his office, his mind still on Lexi and her son.

What had happened in her past? What was it she felt she couldn't tell him? Had she been in love with the boy's father? Had she thought they would be married then he had run out on her? He recalled Jimmy's wide-eyed openness and innocent enthusiasm. It was obvious that Lexi and Jimmy clearly adored each other. He knew in his heart that no matter what past circumstances had shaped the present, she had provided her son with a warm and loving environment. But what did the future hold...for any of them?

For someone who had always known exactly what he

was doing and where he was going, Nick suddenly found himself without a clue. She had asked him so many odd questions. She seemed pleased with his answers, but that didn't explain what was behind it all. He slumped into his desk chair and stared out the office window. The brilliant blue sky enhanced the spectacular mountain scenery. A slight breeze rustled through the trees. Everything looked perfect. So why did he feel so miserable?

He shuffled through some papers on his desk but found it impossible to concentrate on anything. He glanced at the daily activities list. Danny was scheduled to take the afternoon ride. Nick shoved his chair back from his desk and headed for the stables, arriving just after Danny. Nick called to him. "Danny…how about letting me take your afternoon ride?"

His brother eyed him suspiciously. "Why?"

Nick began checking some of the harnesses in an effort to appear busy and avoid eye contact with Danny. "It's a nice day. A ride would be invigorating. Besides, it gives you the afternoon off. I'm sure you must have your eye on one of those lovely ladies who arrived yesterday, the ones sunning themselves out by the pool."

"Well…there is this redhead with big green eyes who sort of grabs me where I live. I'd planned to corner her in the saloon after dinner tonight, but it wouldn't hurt to get a head start."

"All right, then. I'll see you later." Nick watched as Danny left the stables, then turned his attention to preparations for the ride. He threw himself into the physical work in an effort to keep busy, but his thoughts continued to focus on Lexi and her son.

Lexi and Colleen claimed a couple of lounge chairs next to the children's wading pool. The elation she felt

earlier when she concluded that Nick was definitely not
Jimmy's father had been replaced by the disturbing
thoughts at the back of her mind. His expression and tone
of voice told her things were not as settled as she had
wanted to believe.

"Lexi, honey…" Her mother's voice cut into her
thoughts. "Is Jimmy going to be okay in the water by
himself? Should one of us be in the wading pool with him
rather than watching from here?"

"He'll be fine, Mother. Marnie started him on swimming lessons last year and the instructor said he was a
natural. He took to it as if he were born to swim."

She saw the look on her mother's face and knew there
was no way to avoid the upcoming conversation with her
any more than she would be able to avoid it with Nick.

Colleen wasted no more time in getting to what she
wanted to know. "So, tell me what's going on with this
Nick Clayton person. What happens next? I certainly got
the distinct impression that he was not expecting to see
Jimmy and that you haven't even discussed Jimmy with
him. Does this mean you've changed your hard-line position on making him pay?"

Lexi took a calming breath and stared straight ahead as
she filled her mother in on the basic facts. "He's not
Jimmy's father. He didn't even know who Marnie was.
At the time she was in Hawaii, he was in the hospital five
miles down the road with a broken leg and three cracked
ribs." Her information was greeted by silence. She turned
to face her mother and saw Colleen staring blankly toward
the wading pool where Jimmy was playing in the water.

Several seconds passed before Colleen acknowledged
what Lexi had said. "I see." She turned to face her
daughter. "Are you sure about this? He really didn't know
her or he only *claimed* not to know her?"

"After I asked him if he remembered her, he went to their old files and pulled out the publicity photographs taken at that time. He found one with her name on it and recognized her as a previous guest here, but that was it."

"And you believed that?"

"Yes, Mother, I believed what he said."

"What happens now? Do Jimmy and I get on the plane tomorrow morning and go home? Will you be coming with us?"

"I...I don't know. Nick and I still have things to talk about. I...we've...well, we've developed sort of a relationship over the past few days and...well..." She didn't know how to finish her sentence or how much to tell her mother.

Colleen looked quizzically at her. "Are you saying that this man, whom you went out of your way to confront with nearly vendetta-like vehemence about taking responsibility for his son, is not only innocent of the crime, but in a few short days you've managed to develop a close personal *relationship* with him?"

Panic seized Lexi's heart. Intellectually, she knew her mother's questions and comments were logical, but she couldn't answer her yet—not until she and Nick had discussed things first. She didn't want to talk about her relationship with Nick Clayton, about how she'd gotten in over her head with him, only to have everything blow up in her face. She wanted to avoid exposing her personal pain and certainly didn't want to face the inevitable "I told you so" that her mother could deliver so deftly.

"It's nothing, Mother. I was thrown for a loop when I arrived here and discovered things weren't the way I anticipated. That's all there is to it. I just feel that I owe Nick an explanation, or at the very least, an apology for putting him through the third degree concerning his whereabouts when Marnie was in Hawaii.''

''I see,'' Colleen said again, then settled back in her chair, her expression and tone of voice shouting her skepticism.

Lexi concentrated on Jimmy. He had already made friends with another little boy in the pool. They splashed and laughed as they played, without a care in the world. A moment of sadness settled inside her. How marvelous it would be if life were really like that...so open and uncomplicated. For Lexi, what should have been the happiest time of her life had started unraveling before her eyes.

She wondered what Nick was doing. Were his thoughts and feelings as unsettled as hers? In an almost involuntary action, she turned her head in the direction of the stables. She spotted Nick mounting his horse to lead out a riding activity. He had told her the night before that he didn't have any scheduled activities for the next day. Had he chosen to trade with someone in an effort to avoid her? Her spirits sank even lower as the implication hit her.

She had to talk to Nick. She needed answers. Something *was* wrong and it was up to her to clear the air between them. She was the one who had initiated this quest and caused the problem. It was her responsibility to straighten things out...one way or the other. A cold shiver swept up her spine. She hoped the resolution wouldn't be as foreboding as she feared.

Lexi closed her eyes as she leaned back in her lounge chair. Perhaps the warm sun would chase away the ominous chill that had fallen over her.

Nick stepped out of the shower and grabbed a towel. The afternoon ride had done little to take his mind off

Lexi and her son. For all the thought he had given the situation, he had not come up with even a glimmer of insight into this strange turn of events and his feelings surrounding them. It was more than Lexi having a son she hadn't told him about. There were her strange questions about his hospital stay and why that bit of information would be of any importance to her.

He *knew* what was important. He didn't want to lose Lexi. But was he ready to pursue a relationship with a woman who already had a son? Was he prepared to take on the responsibility of an instant family? He didn't know.... He didn't seen to know anything anymore.

He finished drying himself and tossed the towel in the clothes hamper. He stared at himself in the mirror but was unhappy with the image that stared back at him. It was the same man who had always considered himself flexible in new situations and able to adapt to anything. Only this time, he saw a man who needed a swift kick in the seat of his pants to get him moving in the proper direction.

His attention remained riveted on Lexi as he dressed. He needed to find some time alone with her. After asking him some very peculiar questions that morning, she had dismissed him as if everything was fine at long last. The encounter, however, had left him with a number of unanswered questions. Perhaps following dinner, he could separate her from her family long enough for them to have some much needed private time to talk.

He left his cabin and returned to his office. He wanted to take another stab at doing the paperwork he had left earlier that day. Once again he sat at his desk and stared at the mess scattered in front of him. A frown wrinkled his forehead as he slowly shook his head.

"Is everything okay, Nicky?"

He looked up at the sound of his mother's voice, forcing a smile when he saw the worried expression on her face. "Sure. Everything's fine. Why do you ask?"

She wheeled her chair into his office from the hallway. "You had such a pensive look on your face." She paused for a moment as if collecting her thoughts. "Is there a business problem of some sort that you've decided to shoulder by yourself rather than sharing it with the rest of us?"

He forced a nervous chuckle. "Of course not. What makes you ask such a ridiculous question?"

Gloria's expression became stern and her tone of voice quite matter-of-fact. "There's nothing ridiculous about the question. This is exactly what I was talking about the other day. You spend way too much time trying to cover all the bases, being all things to all people, taking all the problems on your own shoulders without sharing any of that load. It's obvious that something's wrong. Now, what is it? Are we being sued by someone? Do we have personnel problems? Are we having difficulty with one of our suppliers? What?"

He rose from his chair and heaved an inner sigh of relief when he realized she was way off base with her assumptions. It helped break the tension that had been building inside him. "If we're experiencing business problems, no one's brought them to my attention." He waved his hand toward the desk. "I was just surprised at how quickly the work had piled up."

"I see. You were so worried about falling behind on the business end of things that you gave Danny the afternoon off and took over his trail ride."

She stared at him, apparently waiting for a reply, but he didn't have a ready one. Things were suddenly closing in around him. Too many things were happening at one time and he didn't know how to juggle the load. It seemed like a long time before he finally answered her challenge. "It's nothing, Mom. Just something I need to work out— a personal matter."

She hesitated a moment, then put forth another question. "Does this have anything to do with Lexi? I saw her leave the pool area a while ago. I assume the woman with her was her mother. And the little boy...who was he?"

"His name is Jimmy." Nick slumped back into his chair. He closed his eyes as he emitted an audible sigh of despair. His brow furrowed in a combination of bewilderment and anguish. "And he's her son."

Ten

Lexi added a touch of lipstick, then checked her appearance in the mirror. She turned to her mother. "Are you ready? They start serving dinner in about ten minutes." She tried to put on an upbeat facade to hide the inner turmoil that had been plaguing her all afternoon. "I hope you're hungry because the food is good and the portions huge."

Colleen glanced around the cabin's interior. "I think so." She picked up her purse and headed for the door.

"Come on, Jimmy. Let's go to dinner." Lexi held out her hand and her nephew ran to her, his grin revealing his missing front tooth and exposing his dimples.

"Are there gonna be cowboys at dinner, Aunt Lexi?"

She smiled at him as she tried to smooth his unruly hair away from his forehead. "I imagine there will be."

Lexi, Colleen and Jimmy walked to the dining hall and found their places at the table. Lexi nervously glanced around the room in an attempt to locate Nick. She finally spotted him hurrying in from the lobby just as dinner was being served. He went directly to the table where he was the host. He shot a quick glance in her direction. She saw the uncertainty on his face and the wariness in his eyes. She continued to watch him for a minute—the smooth manner, the charm that he seemed to put forth with very little effort. To all outward appearances, it would seem that he had no problems or worries.

She turned her attention to her immediate surroundings. She continued to be plagued by uneasy feelings that told her something was very wrong, and she knew what it was. She and Nick had to talk this out. She'd thought the only roadblock to their future had been demolished when she determined that he was not Jimmy's father, but now storm clouds had gathered on the horizon. She knew it was because she had been less than open with the man she'd helplessly fallen in love with. She also knew it was up to her to make things right.

Ken Danzinger, the ranch foreman, acted as host for Lexi's table that evening. The guests at the table engaged in friendly conversation and the food was good. But all through the evening, Lexi stole furtive glances in Nick's direction. Each time she looked his way, she would catch him watching her. And each time it left her struggling with an added dose of apprehension.

Following dinner, Lexi asked her mother to take Jimmy back to the cabin, saying she had some business to take care of. She watched as Colleen took Jimmy's hand and left the dining hall.

Lexi looked around for Nick. She spotted him leaving the dining table headed for the Hoedown Saloon, his stride purposeful and his features displaying an unmistakable intensity. Was he working that evening? This time, she wouldn't fall asleep the way she had the last time he was drafted into service as the bartender. She would join him for that glass of wine. She needed to know if a problem existed or if it was just her imagination. No...she was only kidding herself. There was a problem, all right, and she knew what it was. What she didn't know was how to fix it.

She hurried toward the saloon in an attempt to catch up with Nick. She spotted him having what appeared to be a business conversation with the bartender. Nick handed him a file folder, then a moment later he turned and started toward the exit. She called to him just as he stepped out into the clear night air.

"Nick—wait." She hurried to catch up with him.

She tried to smile warmly, but inwardly she battled the onslaught of panic trying to get a foothold. There was something about his expression, about his body language, that sent a warning signal to her.

There was an awkward moment of silence. She had expected him to take her hand, give it an affectionate squeeze. She had come to look forward to the intimate gesture that had turned into his standard greeting. But it didn't happen. Instead, he stood there, shifting his weight from one foot to the other as if anxious to be on his way.

"What's wrong, Nick? You seem...distracted, as if you have a lot on your mind. Is there anything I can do to help?" She hoped against hope that was the answer—that he was preoccupied with business problems.

Nick shifted his weight again and looked nervously around as if seeking out some sort of distraction. A warning—a portent of something bad—jittered through her body. Her throat tightened and her mouth went dry. She tried to swallow down her panic as she repeated her question.

"Nick? What is it? Are you all right?" Despite her best efforts, she had not been able to keep the alarm out of her voice. Then she saw it in his eyes—the uncertainty that changed to wariness as she watched. She saw him distancing himself from her and backing away, perhaps not physically but certainly emotionally.

It did more than confuse her. It frightened her. Had they reached the end of the line? Could it be that their relationship was nothing more to him than a short-term fling? Had she so completely misjudged this man she thought she knew and had definitely fallen in love with?

She placed a trembling hand on his arm. Her words came out in a frightened whisper. "Nick? Please tell me what's wrong."

Nick had hoped to be able to escape to his office or his cabin, anyplace where he could shut the door and be alone. She had thrown his entire existence into a muddled heap of confusion and doubt. Never in his life had he been so unsure of himself. He desperately needed to work this out, to wrestle with his thoughts and feelings and sort out what was real.

He drew in a steadying breath in an attempt to calm his inner jitters. He raked his fingers through his hair, then rubbed his hand across his nape in an effort to still the uncomfortable shiver. He attempted to swallow down his nervousness, but without much success. The last thing he wanted was to show any outward signs of weakness or vulnerability.

"Uh…you threw me for a loop with Jimmy, that's all. When you asked me what I thought about a woman having a child out of wedlock, I hadn't realized you were talking about yourself. I wish you would have told me earlier that you had a son so I could've been prepared for meeting him rather than you springing him on me like that.''

Her eyes narrowed for a moment, then a hint of something flashed through them. Was it anger? Surely not. She had no right to be angry. She was the one who had been dishonest with him, not the other way around. If anyone was entitled to be angry it was him. She should have come right out and told him about her son as soon as they'd become involved. Why hadn't she? And why had she used such a strange way of hinting at the truth?

He tried to get his confused feelings under control before he said something inappropriate. He wanted very much to hear why she was left to raise her son alone, but on the other hand he was afraid to get more drawn in than he already was. In short, the situation was a mess. He'd never been able to get his head together where Lexi was concerned. Instead of becoming clearer, things turned murkier with each subsequent revelation.

He glanced around searching for something to break the tension that suddenly filled the air. Unsure of exactly what to say to her, he grasped at straws. "Uh…have your mother and your son settled in okay?"

Nick couldn't have hit her harder if he'd actually landed a punch squarely in the middle of her stomach. She felt as if all the breath had been knocked from her body. Had she heard him correctly? Surely not. Her son? She tried to clarify it in her mind, but wasn't getting the pieces to fit together. Could that be it? He was angry because he thought she had a child?

She tried to wrestle with her confused feelings. "I'm not sure I understand exactly what you mean. I threw you for a loop? How did I do that?"

"I simply meant that I think it would've been better if you had told me outright that you had a son rather than dropping obscure hints and asking strange questions,'' Nick said.

She shook her head as she furrowed her brow in confusion. The conversation had taken a very strange and bewildering turn. ''Jimmy is not my son. He's my nephew. He happens to be Marnie's son.'' She tried to swallow the lump that lodged itself in her throat while fighting back a tear. ''She died four months ago and I'm his legal guardian.'' There was no turning back. She had to tell him what she had been trying to hide. She screwed up her courage, fearful of how he might accept what she was about to say. ''I came here for only one reason—to confront you face-to-face and force you to take financial responsibility for your son.''

Her statement literally rocked him on his heels as he took an unsteady step backward. His eyes grew wide and his mouth fell open.

''My what?'' Total disbelief contorted his features and anger filled his voice. ''What the hell are you—''

She cut off his angry response. What she'd feared had become reality. She knew she had to get it all said quickly while she was still able to get out the words. ''From the moment Marnie confided to me that she was pregnant, she steadfastly maintained that you were the father of her child. She said you'd refused to accept any responsibility when she'd told you, that you continued your denials after Jimmy was born. Then you'd told her to stay out of your life, and that you didn't want to hear from her ever again.''

She lowered her voice, unable to keep her pain and anguish hidden away. ''She'd said you were very cold and matter-of-fact about the entire thing. I'd wanted to get an attorney after you, but Marnie begged me to stay out of it. I reluctantly agreed, but when she died and little

Jimmy was left without a mother or a father, I couldn't stand by and do nothing—especially since I held you accountable for her death, as well.''

Nick staggered back a couple more steps, coming to a halt when he bumped into a wall. ''Me?'' His eyes were wide with shock and there was a catch in his voice. ''I didn't even know your sister. How could I have been—''

''Marnie had taken a second job at night. She needed the extra income to provide for Jimmy. She was working for a telephone-answering-and-paging service. The weather that night was miserable. It had been pouring rain all day and there was a lot of flooding. People had been warned to stay off the streets, that driving conditions were too dangerous. I begged her not to go, saying her employer would surely understand. Marnie insisted she had to go. She had only been on the job for a week and didn't want to risk losing it.

''She was caught in a flash flood. Her car stalled out in the water. She apparently left the car and tried to get to safety and find some help, but the strong current swept her away and she drowned.'' Lexi choked back a sob but could not stop the tremors that racked her body as the emotional upheaval she had been trying so hard to suppress finally took control. A tear rolled down her cheek, but she quickly wiped it away.

''She never would've been driving in those treacherous conditions and certainly not on that road at that time if she hadn't been forced to take a second job in order to have enough money to support her son. I swore at her funeral that I would find a way to make you accountable for what you'd done.'' Lexi closed her eyes for a moment to try to stop the tears that threatened to burst loose. ''That was four months ago.''

The last thing she wanted was to show him how much

she was hurting at that moment. She took one calming breath, then another. She looked up at him, finally making eye contact. Nothing was hidden beneath the surface; none of his feelings were concealed. She saw his bewilderment and confusion mixed with a helping of anger and resentment. She also saw the shock that had frozen him into stunned silence. Whatever was going to happen couldn't be stopped now. She needed to tell him everything.

With her initial outburst out of the way, she had recovered a bit of calm. "But when I got here, you were nothing like I'd expected to find. I saw how seriously you took your responsibilities. You were so open and straightforward. I began to question Marnie's story, to wonder what the truth really was. I didn't know what to do or what to think. I considered telling you everything, but if it wasn't true I would only have ended up humiliating you and embarrassing myself.

"Then it occurred to me that perhaps Marnie had not told you about her being pregnant, that you didn't know you had a son. That's why I had to find out where you were. Marnie was in Hawaii at that time. She had mailed me postcards saying you had taken her there. It turned out that was when she became pregnant."

A horrible sinking feeling came over her and refused to leave. Fear churned in her stomach to the point where she thought she might actually be sick. His stance had become adversarial, bordering on defiant. She saw neither compassion nor understanding in his eyes. Instead she saw resentment that sent a cold chill through her body. She desperately needed to say something to defuse the heated situation she had caused before her entire life and future blew up in her face.

She tried to force a smile but all that came out was a

nervous chuckle. "But that's all history now. Obviously, you're not Jimmy's father. This whole thing can be permanently put to rest." Nothing about Nick's expression changed, but his body language told her he had not accepted her attempt to dismiss the problem as no longer relevant.

Nick leveled a cool look at her without averting his gaze for what seemed like an entire minute before he finally said something. His cold, distant tone of voice sent an icy tremor of foreboding through her body. She saw her entire future turning away and she didn't know what to do to stop it. She was more frightened than she had ever been before.

"And just why would your sister accuse me of being the father of her child? I didn't even know her. Beyond the common courtesy of saying good morning in the dining hall at breakfast, there was no connection between us."

Lexi spit out the words in a rush of fear. "I don't know!" She stared at him as she shook her head, her voice dropping to an almost inaudible level. "I just don't know." She furrowed her brow for a moment, as if trying to gather her thoughts into some sort of cohesive, neat little package. "Maybe Jimmy's real father was a married man who had taken her to Hawaii for an extramarital fling. I suppose he could even have been a man she met while she was there. Whoever he was and for whatever reasons, she didn't want to name him as the father."

"But why me? Why would she concoct this lie about me?"

"Again, I don't really know. I can only guess. Perhaps during her stay at the Via Verde she had been attracted to you without your even being aware of it?"

The image of Marnie at his cabin door wearing nothing

but a robe and a smile popped into Nick's head for a second, but he quickly dismissed it. He had sent her away. The isolated incident had nothing to do with the matter at hand.

"When she discovered she was pregnant, she might have picked you as the most responsible man she had ever met and built a fantasy of her own about someone like that being the father of her child. She's the only one who can answer that question, so I guess no one will ever know for sure."

As Lexi was speaking, her voice started to fade into the background. Nick's thoughts were muddled, and he felt as if the bottom of his world had dropped out. He and this woman—Lexi Parker—had made love with a depth of passion that he had never experienced with another woman. She had wandered into his life and turned his entire existence upside down. He had found himself thinking about things that had never been relevant to him before, even to the point of building some sort of future with her. No woman had ever made an impact on his life the way she had. And now he was finding out it had all been a lie. He had never felt so hurt, alone, angry or betrayed in his entire life as he did at that moment.

"So, you arrived here with an ulterior motive and no thought of enjoying a vacation. Your sole purpose was to make me fork over money to support your sister's son. And even after we made love, you allowed me to go on believing that our meeting was by chance, a cowboy and a schoolteacher meeting at a dude ranch and falling into a magic whirl of romance."

He was desperate to keep the hurt out of his voice, but he wasn't sure he had really succeeded. He stretched himself to his full six-one height and tried to project an exterior calm even though it was a long way from what he felt.

"Except now I find out that you made love to me just to get information. For you, there wasn't any romance, and there surely wasn't any magic. Apparently, you're no different from your sister when it comes to deceiving others—" his voice dropped to an almost inaudible level and filled with despair "—like the people who care about you."

The stunned look on her face hurt him almost as much as his words had seemingly hurt her. As soon as they left his mouth, he wanted to call them back, but it was too late. He knew he shouldn't have said what he did. A sharp jab of recrimination cut through his consciousness, but he didn't know what to do or say next.

"Well, if that's the way you feel..." Lexi fought to keep the tears out of her eyes and the catch out of her voice. She wouldn't give him the satisfaction of seeing how devastated she was. "It's better that things end here and now before one of us says or does something else we'll regret for years to come."

She quickly turned her back on him just as the tears edged out of her eyes and streamed down her cheeks. She walked away from the man she loved. She felt as if someone had ripped a hole in her heart. She also knew she had only herself to blame. She should have told him the truth before... Another sob caught in her throat. All the *should have* excuses didn't mean anything. It was too late.

She walked out to the reflecting pond and sat on the bench by the water. She couldn't return to her cabin...not yet. She didn't want to deal with her mother's questions until she could compose herself. And she certainly didn't want to upset Jimmy.

One thing was clear, though. She would be on the shuttle van to the airport the next day. Even if they had to check into a motel for tomorrow night until they caught a flight back to Chicago, she could not stay at Nick Clayton's ranch any longer than necessary.

She shivered. She hugged her shoulders in an attempt to ward off the cold, but it didn't help. Then every bit of self-control she had fought so hard to maintain finally broke loose. She closed her eyes and buried her face in her hands. Spasm after spasm racked her body as the tears flooded down her cheeks. She had never felt so alone as she did at that moment. More than anything, she wanted Nick's arms around her, to be able to draw comfort from his strength, but she knew that would never happen again. The sobs came one after another and she couldn't make them stop.

Nick returned to his cabin. He was having difficulty assimilating what had just happened…beyond the fact that he had stood there like an idiot and allowed Lexi to walk away without making any attempt to stop her. He had said something to her that he knew he would regret for the rest of his life if he couldn't figure out some way to make it right. Yes, she should have told him the truth from the beginning. But then, she had believed her sister. And there was no doubt in his mind that the woman he'd had in his bed was the real, honest Lexi Parker. If only he could turn back the clock and relive the past few hours.

So many things had suddenly become clear to him as he watched her disappear around the corner of the dining hall, not the least of which was the fact that he finally understood that he had fallen totally and completely in love with her. He had tried to deny it, but it had been a useless endeavor and a waste of his time. He knew it was true, just as he knew he might well have thrown away any chance of ever establishing a life together with her.

He took a bottle of beer from the refrigerator, carried it out to the patio as he twisted off the cap, then plopped down into a chair. He had never felt at such a total loss. Handling problems was second nature to him. It was what he did on a daily basis. But he had never come up against a muddle like this one. He had never stood frozen in place and watched in silence as his entire future walked away from him.

Even when his father died and the future of the ranch and the well-being of his mother and brother had been in doubt, he'd known what to do and had taken action. He tried to force his mind into that same sort of logical mode. This was the same type of situation and should be able to be handled in the same way. He would analyze the problem, formulate a plan and put it into action just like any similar type of dilemma.

Unfortunately, there was nothing logical about love. He found himself in the middle of a predicament with no experience to guide him. He didn't have a clue what to do or which way to turn.

So he had stood there like a big dumb idiot and allowed the love of his life to walk away without saying a word.

His thoughts turned to little Jimmy—the wonder that showed on his face as he saw new things; the little boy's curiosity when asking if he was a real cowboy; the missing tooth that showed when he grinned; the wide-eyed innocence that belied the fact that he had already been handed too much tragedy in his young life. There had been something very appealing about this little boy, a truth that touched him much deeper than he had at first suspected or let on.

It had been about family. He recalled his mother's

words that some day he would walk around the corner and there she would be—the woman who would give true meaning to his life, someone with whom he would want to have a family of his own. His mother had been right. He'd looked up from the back of a bucking horse and seen Lexi Parker leaning against the corral fence. He hadn't known who she was or where she had come from, but like a magnet she had drawn him straight to her. Could he really blame her for trying to do right by her sister's son?

As for a family of his own…he frowned as his thoughts took off in another direction.

Jimmy was not his son, regardless of what Lexi had been led to believe. Jimmy was not even Lexi's son. However, he was a child who needed and deserved two loving parents. Could the three of them become a real family, or had they both destroyed that possibility?

He took a swallow from his beer bottle, but the only thing that filled his mouth was the bitter aftertaste of doubt. He had never felt at such a loss over what to do or what to say.

He stiffened to attention as a new determination swept through him. He needed to do what he did best—the direct straightforward approach. Take the bull by the horns and wrestle it to the ground. He had been spending too much time thinking and not enough time doing. He clenched his jaw in determination. He would march over to her cabin, bang on the door and make her listen to him. Things had gotten way out of hand. He would straighten this out right now.

A sigh of desperation escaped his throat as he sank back into the chair. Bulldozing his way in was no solution to his problem and it certainly wouldn't work—not with her mother and Jimmy there. He would have to do something else, but what? He remained slumped in the chair for a couple of minutes. Despair shoved aside any productive thoughts.

Nick finally managed to make his way toward his bedroom even though he knew he would not be getting much sleep that night. He knew something else, too. He knew he was scared. For the first time in his life, he truly feared what the future might hold. For a man who had always been totally in control of his life, he suddenly felt very much out of control.

Eleven

"**I**'m going over to the registration desk, Mother. I want to make sure they have room for us on the shuttle van to the airport this morning." Lexi picked up her sunglasses from the nightstand. "When I get back, we can go over to the dining hall and have breakfast. That should leave us just enough time to pack and check out."

"Can't we stay here, Aunt Lexi?" Jimmy pleaded. "I want to see the horses."

Lexi brushed the hair away from Jimmy's face, then cupped his chin in her hand. She saw the disappointment on his face and it pulled at her heartstrings. So innocent...so trusting. She knew it had been unfair to bring him all the way to Wyoming, introduce him to a fascinating new setting, then not let him stay long enough to enjoy it. But nothing that happened yesterday evening had been fair.

"I'm sorry, honey. We have to leave, but I'll take you

to see some horses when we get home. And we can go to the rodeo next month.'' She tried her best to project an upbeat, enthusiastic tone. ''Would you like that?''

''Yeah, I guess so.'' Jimmy hung his head and turned away without saying anything else.

Lexi wanted to cry. It had been painful enough to have Nick reject her, but she was an adult and would manage to handle it…somehow. But Jimmy… She had seen the way he looked up to Nick, the awe on his little face, the admiration in his voice when he asked if Nick was a real cowboy. It was better to disappoint him now than to have his hero worship crushed by the indifference of this man she had at one time thought she had known so well.

Lexi looked at her mother. ''I'll be back in a little bit.''

The moment Lexi stepped outside, Jimmy dashed toward the door. He pulled it open only seconds after it had closed.

Colleen called to him, ''Jimmy…where are you going?''

''I'm going with Aunt Lexi, Grandma.'' Then he was out the door.

Jimmy stood outside the cabin and looked around. Lexi was nowhere in sight. The horses in the corral quickly drew his attention and he forgot all about going with Lexi. The little boy ran over to the corral and tried to climb up on the fence, but he was too small. He peered through the railings and watched the horses for several minutes, then spotted Nick entering the stables.

Nick removed his hat and hung it on a hook just inside the stable door. He took his leather work gloves from his belt and pulled them on. He had plenty to do, but no enthusiasm for the job. He had tossed and turned the entire night, getting maybe a total of two hours' sleep. As if to confirm his assessment, he stifled a yawn. He went to the tack room, poured a mug of steaming coffee, then carried it back into the stables.

He stopped short when he saw the little boy standing in the horse-grooming area looking around as if trying to get his bearings. Once again, the display of wide-eyed wonder tugged at Nick's senses. For a little boy who had never known a father and at the tender age of five had lost his mother, he seemed to be well-adjusted. Marnie had apparently done a good job of raising her son. And now the responsibility had passed on to Lexi.

He had spent the entire night trying to figure out what to say to Lexi. Nothing had jelled in his mind; no plan of action had presented itself. He realized he'd better come up with something soon or it might be too late.

"Can I pet the horses?"

The little boy's voice cut into Nick's thoughts, followed by a gentle tugging on his shirtsleeve. He looked down to see Jimmy standing next to him. He dropped to one knee so he wouldn't tower over the boy.

"Are you here all alone?" A flicker of hope ignited inside him. He quickly scanned the area looking for Lexi, but his spirits fell when he didn't see her anywhere.

Jimmy repeated his question. "Can I pet the horses?"

Nick felt uneasy. He was alone with this child and felt at a loss for words. "Uh…well, yes…I guess it would be okay."

Jimmy grinned at him, exposing the gap where his front tooth used to be. And at that moment, Nick Clayton's fears melted away. This little boy who had weathered so many upsets in his young life had totally captivated him.

"Which one is your horse?" The excitement sparkled in Jimmy's eyes. "Can I pet him?"

Nick returned Jimmy's grin. "I'll tell you what, partner. Let's find a horse more your size."

Almost involuntarily, Nick grabbed his hat from the hook and put it on Jimmy's head. Then he held out his hand and Jimmy grasped it. The two of them walked to the far end of the long building where the Shetland ponies were stabled. One of the ponies poked its head through the gate railing. Jimmy's eyes grew wide and he jumped back to safety, hiding behind Nick's leg. He tentatively took a step forward and reached out with his hand, but when the pony shook its head, he quickly withdrew. He looked up at Nick, the questioning expression on his face asking if he had done something wrong.

"It's okay, Jimmy. This is Coco and she was just saying hello to you." He placed his hand on the pony's neck and gently stroked. "Pet her like this."

Jimmy hesitantly reached out, but this time he didn't pull back when Coco shook her head. His hand touched the pony's neck, then he began to stroke her as Nick had shown him. His entire face lit up and he beamed with excitement.

Nick reached into a bucket and retrieved a freshly cut piece of carrot. He handed it to Jimmy. "Coco loves carrots. Put this in the palm of your open hand and hold it out for her."

Jimmy followed Nick's instructions. When the pony took the treat from his hand, Jimmy giggled with delight. He looked up at Nick. "Can I do it again?"

"Sure." Nick handed him another piece of carrot. "Would you like to go for a ride on Coco?"

Jimmy looked up at Nick, his eyes filled with wonderment. He spoke in hushed tones, as if he couldn't believe what was happening. "Could I do that?"

"Of course you can. We'll put a saddle on her and—"

"Jimmy!" Lexi called frantically from the front of the

stables, her voice carrying the distinct overtones of panic. "Are you in here?"

"Lexi?" Nick responded to her entreaty, calling to her from the back of the stables. "He's here with me." He took Jimmy's hand and they headed toward the sound of Lexi's voice. As they drew close to her, he could see how distraught she was. "Is something wrong?"

She rushed toward them, relief showing on her face and in her voice. She ignored Nick and knelt next to Jimmy. "I've been looking everywhere for you. Grandma thought you were with me, but I didn't know where you'd gone. Are you okay?"

"Oh, sure." A big grin spread across Jimmy's face. Nick's many-sizes-too-big cowboy hat slid across his forehead and settled against his nose. Jimmy pushed it back so he could see but continued to hold on to it when Lexi tried to take it off his head. "Nick let me pet a horse...a little horse, just my size. Her name is Coco. Nick says he'll take me for a ride on Coco. Can I go? Please, Aunt Lexi? Please?"

Lexi threw a sidelong glance at Nick showing her displeasure, then returned her attention to Jimmy. She tried to swallow down the lump in her throat and project an outward calm. "Nick's a very busy man, Jimmy. We need to let him get back to his work." Once again, she saw the disappointment on Jimmy's face and it tugged at her emotions. He asked for so little, but she had to say no to this.

"I'm not busy. I have plenty of time to take Jimmy for a ride." Nick had rushed his words, but he wanted to get them in before Lexi said anything else.

Lexi rose to her feet and took Jimmy's hand. "Well, I'm afraid we don't have time. We need to pack."

"Pack?" Tension jabbed at Nick's insides. "Where are you going? You booked in for a three week stay. Jimmy and your mother just arrived yesterday. Surely you can't be leaving so soon.''

"We're taking the shuttle van to the airport." She turned her attention to Jimmy again. "You'll have to give Nick's hat back to him now so we can go.''

She saw yet another look of disappointment cross Jimmy's face as he handed the prized cowboy hat back to its owner. Her heart sank. She was beginning to feel like the wicked stepmother in the story of Cinderella.

She addressed an expressionless comment to Nick. "If you'll excuse us, we have lots to do." She turned to leave, but Nick immediately brought her to a halt by grabbing her arm.

"You can't go." He fought back the desperation that swept over him. "We...we need to talk." He didn't have anything prepared to say, but he knew he couldn't let her walk away again without trying to stop her. He directed a friendly smile toward Jimmy. "Would you like to go pet Coco again? Your aunt Lexi and I will wait here for you.''

Lexi held tight to Jimmy's hand so he couldn't leave. No good could come from this sudden reaching out on Nick's part. She lowered her voice to a whisper. "I don't know what you're trying to prove by this sudden display. I believe you said everything there was to say yesterday.'' She fought to keep the quaver out of her voice. "I can't imagine what else there could be to discuss.''

And once again, Nick Clayton stood glued to the spot and watched helplessly as Lexi Parker walked out the door...and out of his life?

"That was certainly an interesting display of stupidity, and I'm not referring to Lexi.''

Nick whirled around at the sound of the voice and spotted Danny leaning against the tack-room doorjamb, a cup of coffee in his hands. He glared at his brother. "How long have you been standing there?" He clipped his words, partly in anger and partly to cover his embarrassment at having someone witness his colossal show of idiocy.

"Long enough to see you make a fool of yourself." Danny straightened up and sauntered over to Nick. "I don't know what happened to cause this rift between you two, but I do know that you're never going to find a woman more right for you than she is."

Nick tried to dismiss Danny's comments. "It's nothing...you wouldn't understand."

"Maybe I would if you told me about it. I do know what I've seen over the past few days and it looked to me like the two of you were well on your way to something permanent."

Nick angrily snapped out a response. "Well, you were wrong." He leaned back against a stall railing and took a calming breath. His voice dropped almost to a monotone, as if he had just been overwhelmed by the obvious. "I have too many responsibilities already, Danny. I have the ranch and all its employees depending on me to keep things going. And those employees depend on that paycheck for their livelihood. And there's Mom's health. She was just in the hospital—"

"Let's start with that. I don't know how many doctors need to tell you that Mom's health is just fine before you'll believe it. And as for the ranch...you're trying to be a one-man show, Nick. The truth is that this operation has grown too large for you to oversee every little detail. You're going to drive yourself crazy if you continue to try to be everywhere at once."

"Your argument is no good. Every time something happens, it ends up being dumped in my lap, just like that situation with Tony. I can't turn my back on that and ignore it.''

"No, but what you can do is to start delegating some of that authority. I could easily take on more responsibility and lighten your load. But it can't happen if you refuse to let go of some of those responsibilities and share that load. The ranch is doing great financially. You could even hire a resort manager to take care of all the day-to-day problems.''

"Well...yes, I suppose I could look into that.'' Nick's voice grew hesitant as he tried to digest Danny's clearly well-intentioned and surprisingly well-thought-out suggestions.

"You've got to stop putting everything and everybody first and yourself second. You need to get a life of your own before it's too late.'' Danny grinned. "You're not getting any younger, you know.''

A soft chuckle of resignation escaped Nick's throat as he regarded his younger brother. "It seems that sometime over the past few years you managed to grow up while I wasn't looking.''

"So maybe you'd better talk to Lexi before it's too late. She made arrangements this morning for the three of them to leave on the shuttle van for the airport. That's why I came here looking for you, to see if you knew she was leaving.''

"No, I didn't know until she told me a few minutes ago.'' Nick shoved his hands into his pockets and stared at the ground. "It's not that easy. I can ask her to stay, but what am I offering her? How can I do that when I don't know what I want?''

Danny took a sip of his coffee. "You'd better hurry up and figure it out or she'll be gone.''

Nick left the stables. Everything Danny had said was

true. He could make more time in his life by putting more responsibility for the business on Danny's shoulders and even hiring a manager. That would allow him to pursue a personal life separate from the ranch. But it still brought him around to the same old question—exactly what did he want?

For Nick Clayton, working out a problem meant some type of physical activity. He went out to the corral looking for Ken Danzinger. "Have someone saddle up Tempest for me."

Ken looked at him curiously. "That horse has thrown you every time you've gotten on his back."

The weariness of a man who had the weight of the world on his shoulders settled over Nick. He heaved a sigh, mumbling a response rather than giving thought to Ken's concern. "Maybe I'll get lucky this time. Or maybe I'll end up breaking my neck."

One of the wranglers saddled Tempest and led the bronco into the chute. Nick climbed the fence and carefully eased himself onto the horse's back. He felt the horse shift nervously under him. He took a steadying breath, tightened the rope around his hand, then nodded at Ken to open the chute. Before he could even catch his breath, he found himself flying through the air, then rolling in the dirt.

For the better part of an hour, Nick tried again and again to stay on for a full ride, and each time he ended up on the ground. It was the same horse that had thrown him on his rear end the day Lexi had first stood at the corral railing watching him. It seemed like such a long time ago. So much had happened since then.

He picked himself up once more, made a futile attempt at brushing some of the dirt from his clothes and slowly made his way across the corral. He felt a twinge of pain in his leg but refused to favor it. He had overdone it again. It was the leg he had broken before, and every now and then it objected to excessive abuse such as the kind he had just heaped on it.

He headed for the water jug. Just as he reached for it, Danny snatched it up and handed it to him. Nick shot Danny an irritated look as he took the jug from him. "Don't you have something better to do than hanging around watching me?" he snapped out angrily.

Danny allowed a mischievous grin. "Nope, not at the moment."

Nick took a long swig of cold water, then poured some of it over his head in the hopes that it would cool him off. He regarded Danny for a moment, taking note of the fact that his brother didn't seem to be making any effort to leave.

Danny eased himself away from the fence railing and stood face-to-face with Nick. "Do you think you've punished yourself enough yet?"

"I don't know what you're talking about. I've been trying to ride Tempest ever since we got him. Today's no different."

"If you say so." Danny's tone said he didn't believe a word Nick had said. He started to turn away, then halted in his tracks. He fixed Nick with a hard stare. "The shuttle van will be leaving for the airport in less than half an hour, and as far as I can tell, Lexi plans to be on it. Is that the way you want it to be?" Danny didn't wait for an answer. He walked off, leaving Nick standing by the corral fence.

Nick wiped the water out of his eyes with his shirt-sleeve, managing to add yet another dirty smudge to his face. He glanced over at the front drive. Herb had pulled the shuttle van around to the lobby door and would be loading luggage before long. A mass of doubts churned inside him. He knew what he had to do but didn't have any idea how to go about it. And time was running out.

He could not allow her to leave, not now, and certainly not under these circumstances. But first, he needed to take a shower and put on some clean clothes. He started for his cabin, his thoughts totally muddled and his nerve endings exposed and raw.

Lexi placed the last of her clothes in the suitcase and closed the lid. She looked around the cabin, searching for anything she might have overlooked. She placed her cases by the cabin door next to Colleen's and Jimmy's.

"I think that's everything, Mother." It certainly was everything. Her clothes…and any chance of future happiness. She knew in her heart that she would never love another man as much as she loved Nick Clayton.

The knock at her cabin door—more like someone pounding with a fist—intruded into her glum thoughts. She pulled open the door.

A sudden intake of breath accompanied her surprise at the sight that greeted her. A totally disheveled Nick Clayton stood in front of her, a thousand uncertainties wavering across his face. This dirty and sweaty man was far removed from the self-confident cowboy she'd seen when she first arrived at the ranch.

"Could we talk—" he peered over her shoulder at Colleen and Jimmy "—maybe out here where we can have some privacy?" His every word and gesture said he was a man attempting to find his way in totally unfamiliar territory.

"Uh…Lexi…I think I'll take Jimmy to get some ice cream." Colleen took her grandson's hand and started for the door, her demeanor saying she wanted to get away from whatever was about to happen. Nick stepped aside so they could leave, then entered the cabin and shut the door behind him.

A sinking feeling left a hard lump in the pit of Lexi's stomach. He reached out for her, but she deftly side-stepped his attempt. She nervously cleared her throat. "I can't imagine what you're doing here, but please be quick about it. I need to get the luggage out to the van."

He hadn't had a clue as to what he was going to say when he knocked at her door. He had gotten halfway to his cabin when a panic attack seized him. He abruptly turned and raced toward her cabin. All he could think about was that he might be too late. He knew the shuttle van hadn't left yet, so she was still at the ranch, but did he still have enough time to reach her? And would she listen to him?

He tried to sound composed and sure of himself, but he knew he wasn't doing a very good job of it. "You can't leave...not yet...not like this."

Nick saw the anger flash in Lexi's eyes, but he also saw the hurt underneath it. Her stance may have been aggressive, her words strong, but he heard the uncertainty in her voice. "Far be it from me to dispute your opinion, but in this case I'm afraid you're wrong. I most certainly can leave and fully intend to just as soon as you get out of my way."

He reached out for her again, this time managing to pull her into his arms. She struggled at first, then seemed to relent a bit as she allowed him to draw her into his embrace. He held her head against his shoulder, stroked her hair and emitted a sigh that came out part despair and part relief.

"I'm sorry, Lexi. I'm so very sorry. I said things I shouldn't have...things I didn't mean." It felt so good to have her in his arms again. "You caught me completely by surprise and I reacted like an idiot. I don't understand why you went through all the subterfuge. Why didn't you just come right out and ask me about it?"

The jitters that had invaded her body the moment she saw him at the door began to subside. It felt so good to have his arms around her again, so comfortable…so very right. Did she dare hope that they could salvage something from all of this mess?

"Marnie said if I confronted you, like I wanted to do the moment she'd told me about it, you'd just deny it. I assumed she was right, that it wouldn't accomplish anything. I thought the best thing to do would be to find out what kind of person you were so I would be able to anticipate what you'd do, sort of get into your head."

He cupped her face in his hands and looked into her eyes. She placed her hands on top of his. "I would never fault anyone for taking responsibility and trying to do the right thing. And I guess I really can't blame you for the way you followed through in trying to take care of Jimmy and find his father." He placed a tender kiss on her lips, then cradled her head against his shoulder again. His words came out as a soft whisper. "Don't leave, Lexi. I want you to stay."

Only two little sentences, but they bounced around inside her head loud and clear. They raised her spirits a hundredfold, but then she floated back to earth and reality. He had asked her to stay but had not offered any type of commitment. Once again she was left wondering what type of relationship they had. Only this time she would not let it remain an unasked question.

"Stay? For how long? Until my three weeks are up? Until it's time for me to go back to work? You'll have to tell me what you mean, Nick. I don't want to make the same mistake again. I don't want to assume something that isn't so."

The response she anticipated didn't materialize. She waited, hoping he would say what she wanted to hear...that he wanted her to stay permanently, that he loved her, that he wanted them to be married. But he said nothing. With a heavy heart, she pulled out of his embrace. She couldn't look at him. She knew everything she felt at that second showed on her face and in her eyes.

"I see." She couldn't hide the disappointment that crept into her voice. "I guess your silence says it all. I'd better find Mother and Jimmy." She picked up her purse and opened the cabin door. She thought she had cried out every tear possible last night while sitting next to the reflecting pond. But she had been wrong. She felt the tears well in her eyes. She fought to keep them back.

So, this was how it would end after all. She had asked for a commitment, but he hadn't given her one. She loved him, but he didn't love her. She would go back to Chicago, return to her job, and for the rest of her life would compare every man she met with Nick Clayton and find each of them lacking.

She forced as much confidence into her voice as she could muster. "Goodbye, Nick." She stepped outside.

A horrible pain ripped through his emotions. He saw her walking away from him. It was the third time, and he knew if he didn't do something now she would be lost to him forever. The words came out of his mouth at the same time as they formed in his mind.

"Lexi! Don't go!" He called to her, perhaps more loudly than he'd intended, but he was scared. "I love you." Once the words were spoken, it was as if all the cares of the world had suddenly been whisked away. He felt so free and unafraid. Was it too late?

I love you. The words went straight to her heart. She whirled around. It was true. She saw it on his face and in his eyes. It was what she had longed to hear.

His clothes were a disheveled mess. He was sweaty and had dirty smudges on his face. He was badly in need of a shower. At that moment, he was not a larger-than-life fantasy. He was a very real man who stood before her with his vulnerability exposed. He was life itself. And he was everything she had ever wanted.

Her voice quavered as she started to speak. "Do you really?"

He went to her, holding out his arms until he was able to enfold her in his embrace. "With all my heart I mean it.

"I love you, too, Nick. I love you very much."

"It took me a while to figure out what I wanted, but now I know what it is." He placed a loving kiss on her lips before continuing. "You came here looking for Jimmy's father and you found him. Not his biological father, but certainly the man to give Jimmy a stable home." He brushed another kiss across her lips, then took a steadying breath. "I love you, Lexi, and I want us to be a real family." A teasing grin tugged at the corners of his mouth. "Besides, don't you think two people named Nicholas and Alexandra really ought to spend their lives together?"

The happiness that swelled her heart far surpassed what she had ever imagined. They would be a family, a real family. Even have children of their own someday. She looked up at him, tears of joy filling her eyes. "If that's a proposal…I accept."

*   *   *   *   *

SILHOUETTE® Desire®

continues the captivating series from
bestselling author **Maureen Child**

BACHELOR BATTALION

*Defending their country is their duty;
love and marriage is their reward!*

December 1999: **MARINE UNDER THE MISTLETOE
(SD#1258)**

It took only one look for Marie Santini to fall head over heels for
marine sergeant Davis Garvey. But Davis didn't know if he was
capable of loving anyone. Could a Christmas miracle show him the
true meaning of love?

If you missed any of the books in the Bachelor Battalion series,
act now to order your copy today!

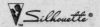

Start celebrating Silhouette's 20th anniversary
with these 4 special titles by
New York Times bestselling authors

Fire and Rain
by Elizabeth Lowell

King of the Castle
by Heather Graham Pozzessere

State Secrets
by Linda Lael Miller

Paint Me Rainbows
by Fern Michaels

On sale in December 1999

Available at your favorite retail outlet

Silhouette®

Visit us at www.romance.net

PSNYT

LINDSAY McKENNA
continues her heart-stopping series:

MORGAN'S MERCENARIES
III
THE HUNTERS

Coming in October 1999:
HUNTER'S PRIDE
Special Edition #1274

Devlin Hunter had a way with the ladies, but when it came to his job as a mercenary, the brooding bachelor worked alone. Then his latest assignment paired him up with Kulani Dawson, a feisty beauty whose tender vulnerabilities brought out his every protective instinct—and chipped away at his proud vow never to fall in love....

Coming in January 2000:
THE UNTAMED HUNTER
Silhouette Desire #1262

Rock-solid Shep Hunter was unconquerable—until his mission brought him face-to-face with Dr. Maggie Harper, the woman who'd walked away from him years ago. Now Shep struggled to keep strong-willed Maggie under his command without giving up the steel-clad grip on his heart....

Look for Inca's story when Lindsay McKenna continues the MORGAN'S MERCENARIES series with a brand-new, longer-length single title—coming in 2000!

Available at your favorite retail outlet.

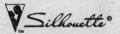

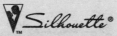